PARANORMAL SCIENCE NVL

Occultic;Nine
オカルティック・ナイン

THERE IS NO SUCH THING AS THE "OCCULT." IT CAN ALL BE DISPROVED BY SCIENCE.
ONLY THOSE WHO HAVE ACCEPTED EVERYTHING
HAVE THE RIGHT TO KNOW THE TRUTH.

03

CHIYOMARU SHIKURA

art by **pako**

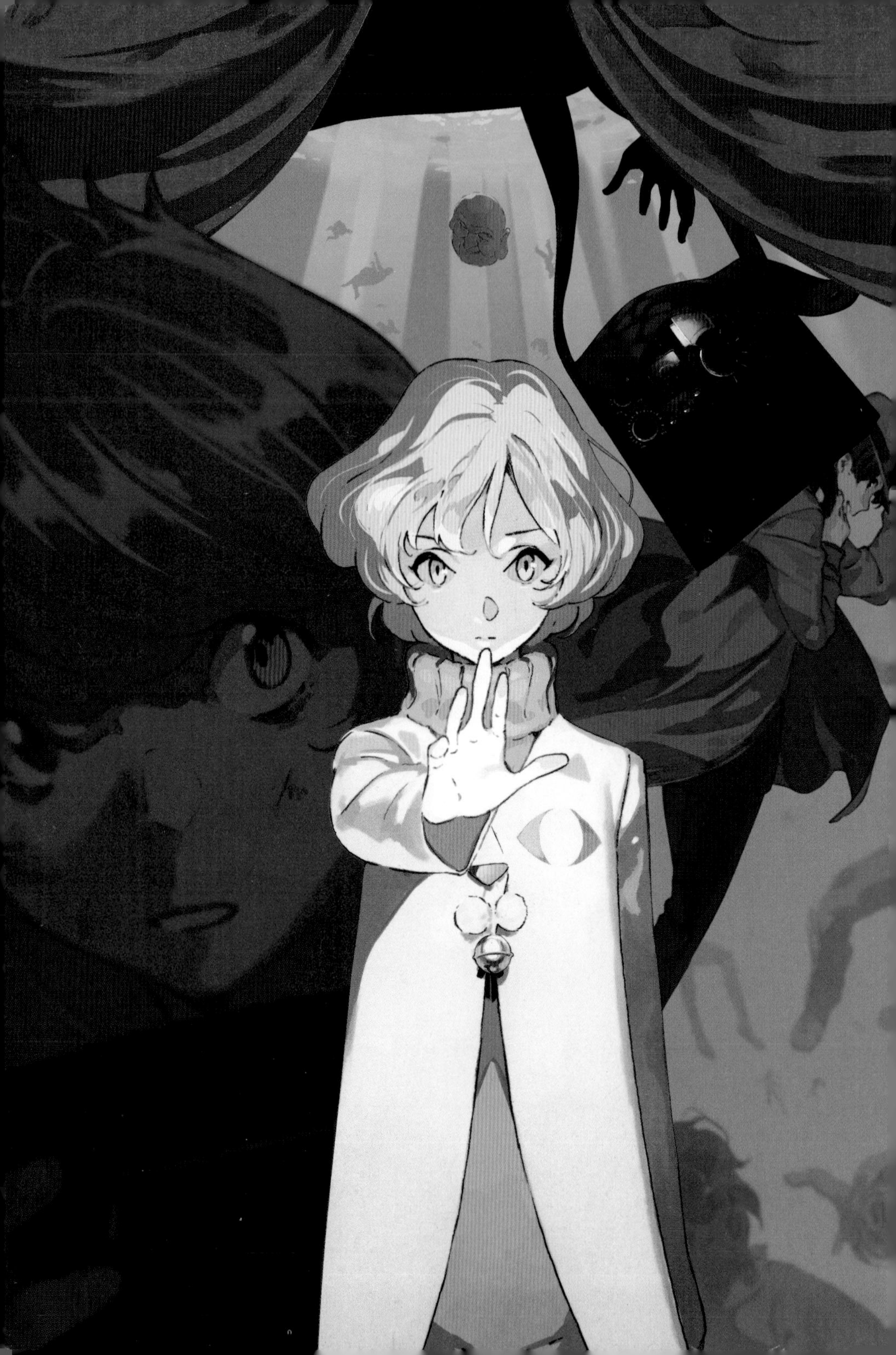

"Kizaki?"

"...?"

Suddenly I heard my name from behind me and turned around. One of my classmates, a girl with her hair in long braids, was standing there.

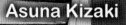

Asuna Kizaki

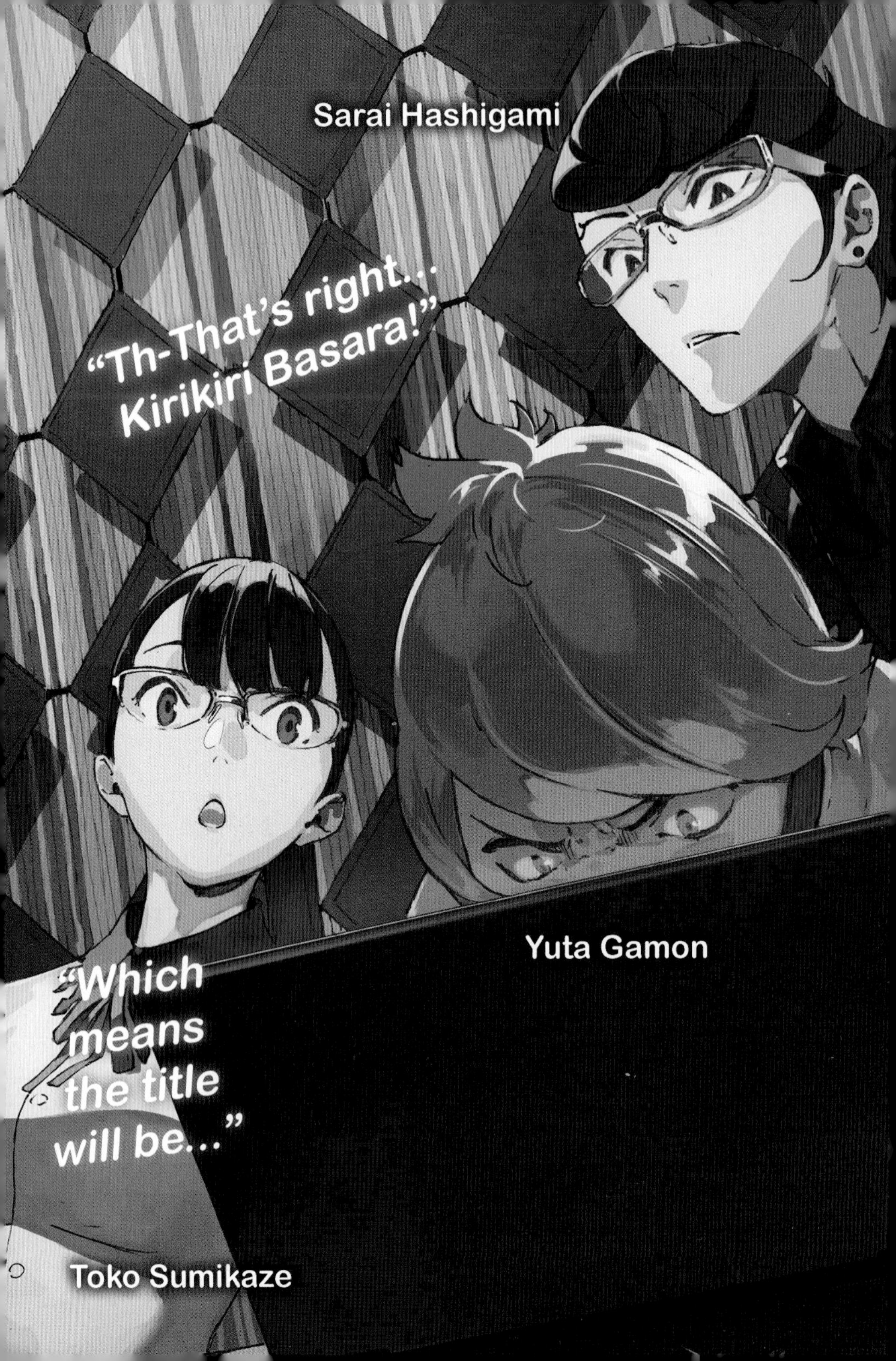
Sarai Hashigami
"Th-That's right… Kirikiri Basara!"
Yuta Gamon
"Which means the title will be…"
Toko Sumikaze

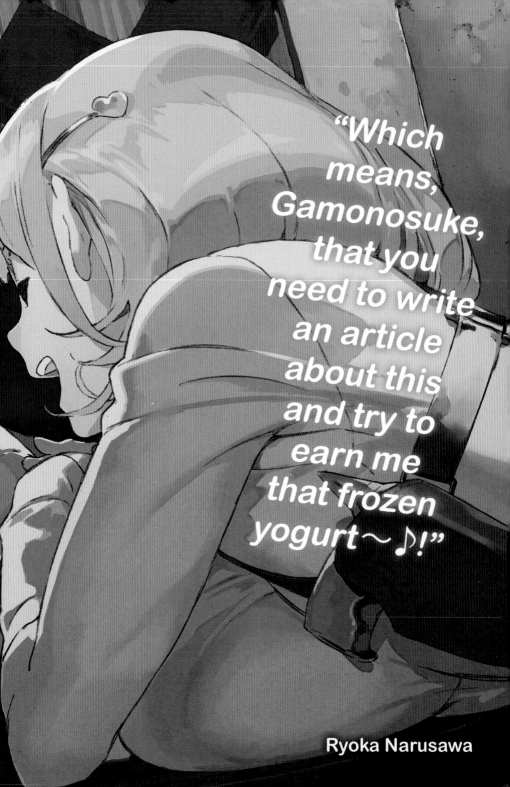

"Which means, Gamonosuke, that you need to write an article about this and try to earn me that frozen yogurt~ ♪!"

Ryoka Narusawa

"Th-That's me..."

I heard a voice in front of me. I looked up, and standing there was a boy who looked exactly like the corpse I'd just touched in the coffin.

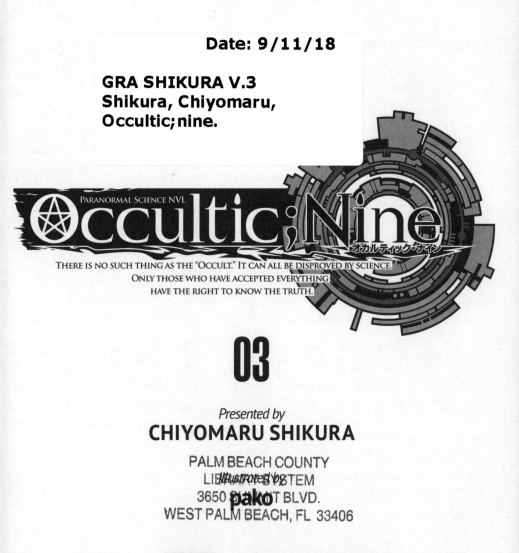

PARANORMAL SCIENCE NVL

Occultic;Nine

オカルティック・ナイン

THERE IS NO SUCH THING AS THE "OCCULT." IT CAN ALL BE DISPROVED BY SCIENCE.
ONLY THOSE WHO HAVE ACCEPTED EVERYTHING
HAVE THE RIGHT TO KNOW THE TRUTH.

03

Presented by
CHIYOMARU SHIKURA

Illustrated by
pako

Seven Seas

novel
club

OCCULTIC;NINE, VOLUME 3

© 2015 SHIKURA CHIYOMARU
Illustrations by pako

First published in Japan in 2017 by
OVERLAP Inc., Ltd., Tokyo.
English translation rights arranged with
OVERLAP Inc., Ltd., Tokyo.

Seven Seas books may be purchased in bulk for promotional,
educational, or business use. Please contact your local
bookseller or the Macmillan Corporate and Premium Sales
Department at 1-800-221-7945, extension 5442, or by
e-mail at MacmillanSpecialMarkets@macmillan.com.

Follow Seven Seas Entertainment online at
sevenseasentertainment.com.
Experience J-Novel Club books online at j-novel.club.

TRANSLATION: Adam Lensenmayer
J-NOVEL EDITOR: Sasha McGlynn
COVER DESIGN: Nicky Lim
INTERIOR LAYOUT & DESIGN: Jamie Goldkamp
COPY EDITOR: Dayna Abel
PROOFREADER: Stephanie Cohen
ASSISTANT EDITOR: Jenn Grunigen
LIGHT NOVEL EDITOR: Nibedita Sen
EDITOR-IN-CHIEF: Adam Arnold
PUBLISHER: Jason DeAngelis

ISBN: 978-1-626926-63-9
Printed in Canada
First Printing: July 2018
10 9 8 7 6 5 4 3 2 1

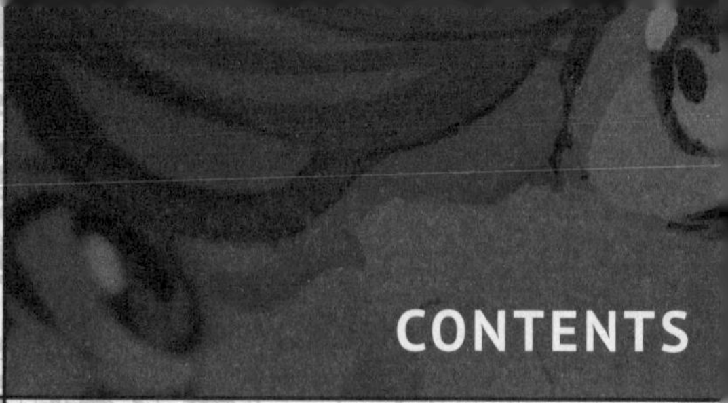

CONTENTS

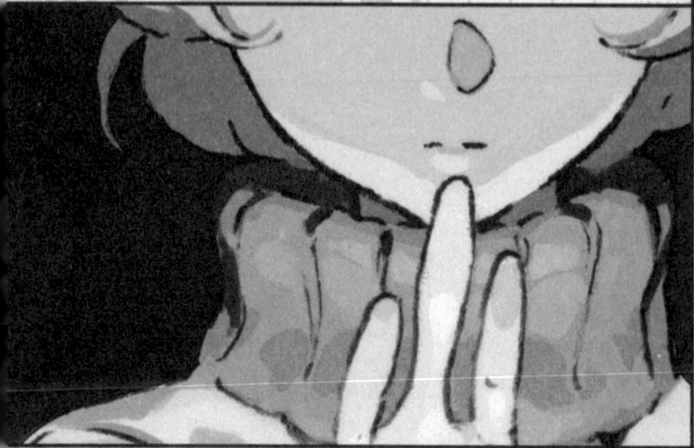

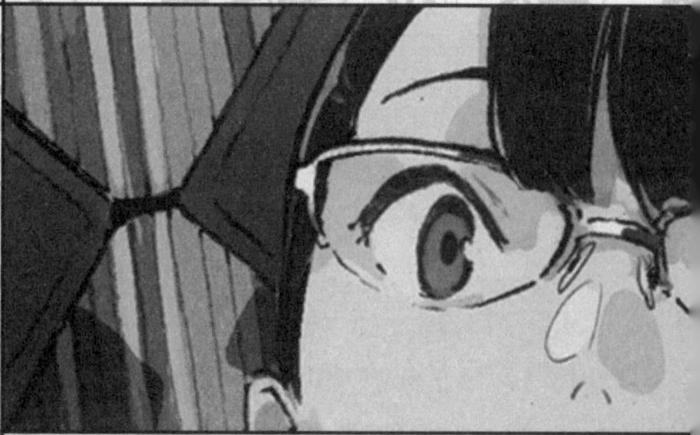

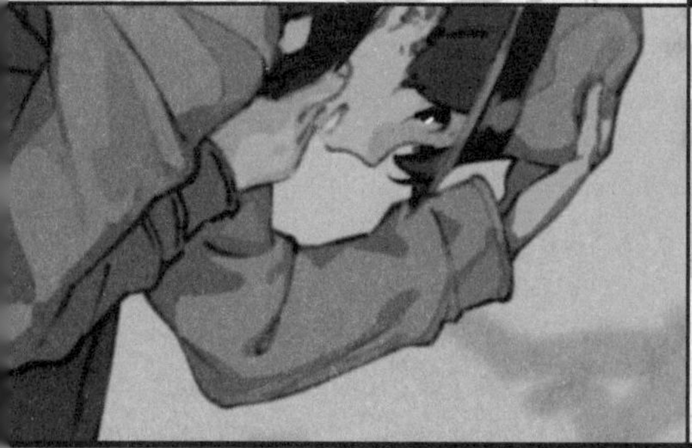

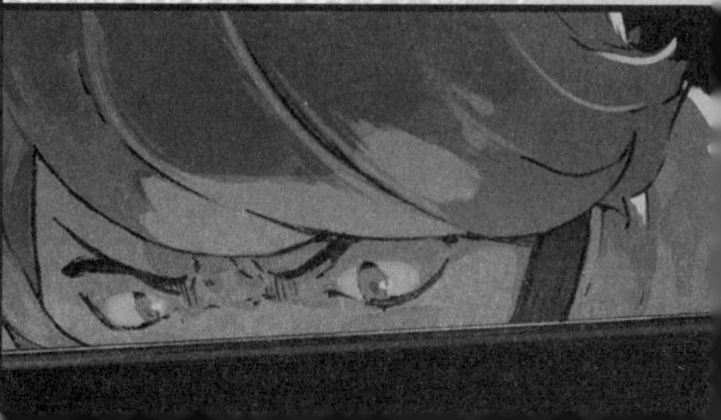

Occultic;Nine
PARANORMAL SCIENCE NVL

THERE IS NO SUCH THING AS THE "OCCULT." IT CAN ALL BE DISPROVED BY SCIENCE.
ONLY THOSE WHO HAVE ACCEPTED EVERYTHING
HAVE THE RIGHT TO KNOW THE TRUTH.

Bzzzzzt bbzzzzzt...

The only thing coming from the Skysensor now was static.

That's how Zonko always was. She'd just show up, say something, and then go silent without giving me any answers. She wouldn't answer any questions I had at all. That was what I hated about her.

"Why aren't you saying something? Is this one of those shows where they have a mystery and say, 'We'll reveal the answer right after these commercials!'?"

Those shows never revealed the answer after the break. You usually had to wait until the next week. Stuff like that was really frustrating.

Still feeling stunned, I turned back towards the TV screen. The news was still reporting on the same story.

They said that the casualties from the 256 Incident were gradually being identified. Two hundred had been found. The names of the victims—I didn't know if that was the right word, since they might have been suicides—scrolled across the screen in alphabetical order. I read each one in turn, forgetting to breathe. Maybe I'd only imagined hearing my own name.

Twenty names were being displayed on the screen at a time. The announcer would read each one, then the screen went on to the next twenty. The wait was agonizing. I realized my throat was parched. I told myself it was stupid to get this nervous, but I couldn't take my eyes off the screen.

After a few more sets of names, I found it again.

"Yuta Gamon."

There was no mistaking it. The name was right there.

"Breaking news!" I shouted. "It turns out…I'm definitely dead!" I found myself standing up and dancing for no reason. "Wahoo!"

I'd seen mistaken broadcasts like this turn into a big deal online a bunch of times, but I never thought it would happen to me. This could be one of the biggest stories of my life. If anything, I wanted to update the blog right away.

Then again, that would have meant putting my real name online, so no way that was happening!

"Man, talk about an LOL. This may even qualify as an ROFLMAO, it's so weird."

One of the victims of the 256 Incident had the same name I did. Talk about a strange coincidence. I couldn't make too big a deal out of it, though. It wouldn't be fair to the other Yuta Gamon.

"Or maybe I'm the one who died…nah, that's impossible!"

I mean, I was watching TV right now, and the incident happened days ago. I'd been alive like normal then. I was doing stuff like going to Café Blue Moon and drinking Master Izumin's nasty tea, or updating Kirikiri Basara. Then after Sarai had chased me, I'd gone to his house and found the encoded list hidden in his ceiling. After that, I'd been there to see what happened to Myu-Pom's friend. I remembered hearing her scream. It was a scream filled with despair that still echoed in my ears.

"Ugh."

I remembered the scraps of red flesh in the wooden box and put my hand over my mouth. Myu-Pom seemed sure about what they were... But they sure didn't look human to me. There was so little left that it was impossible to tell what it was. There was no way that could have been a person—and who was that pale boy who'd escaped?

It wasn't that I couldn't believe it, it was just... Yeah. It was impossible. The one thing I did remember, though, was the awful smell.

"And since remembering that smell makes me want to throw up, that means I'm alive. Q.E.D."

Who cares if my name was on TV? Who cares if my name was on Dr. Hashigami's list? It made a lot more sense to think that somebody with my name had been killed instead of me.

It did, right? I mean, that explained why the name appeared on both lists.

"........."

I started to feel really cold all of a sudden and began to pace around the room.

"This is all because Zonko won't tell me anything!"

I decided to start by proving I was alive.

That was easy. I could just pinch my cheek.

"Owww!"

It hurt! That really hurt! "I've proven I'm alive! Q.E.D.! Q.E.D.!" There, that settled that.

No, wait. I needed more. I wanted more proof that I was alive. Maybe it would be better for my mental health if I went somewhere instead of just sitting in my room all day.

"I'll go ask Mom." I walked out of the room on shaking, unsteady legs.

The calendar said it was spring, but the living room was freezing cold. Did somebody leave the air conditioner on? I rubbed my arms to warm myself up, but it didn't do any good.

"Well, you know what this means, right? If I feel cold, it's because I'm alive," I said to no one in particular, but in my mind I was thinking something else.

Is it cold because I'm dead?

If that was the case, then maybe it didn't mean I was alive. Maybe I was just trying to run from reality.

No, no, no. That's overthinking it.

"Mom?" I called out, but there was nobody in the living room. "Oh, I guess she'd be out at this hour."

Mom was always busy at work. She left earlier in the morning than I did, and she didn't get back until very late. Sometimes I thought she might be a workaholic.

I thought it would be easy to prove I was alive, but I'd already run into a stumbling block.

Grr…what now?

"I know! The phone!" I called my mom's number on my cellphone. If I could place phone calls, that meant I was alive. Yet another Q.E.D.! But just in case, I wanted to hear my mom's voice.

"………"

The ringing sound was quickly replaced with an answering machine. She was at work, and she wouldn't pick up at this hour. There was nothing unusual about that, but…

This was getting frustrating. I wanted something that would give me solid, unassailable proof.

At this point, I'd just have to go outside.

"Okay, I'll go to Blue Moon!"

Master Izumin and Ryotasu should both be there. Maybe Sarai would be there, too. If I could see them and talk to them, that would prove it!

Proving that you're alive is surprisingly difficult, I thought to myself as I left the house. I wanted to see somebody's face so badly that I was willing to drink one of Master Izumin's "lucky drinks" if I had to.

"Ugh."

I went outside, my eyes squinting in the spring sunlight. The sun was dazzlingly bright. Somehow, this made me feel so much safer. It was cold in the house, but the sunlight was warm.

After what had happened with Myu-Pom, it felt like the only thing I could do was work on decoding the list, so it had been a long time since I'd left the house. I hadn't slept that much, either. For that matter, I couldn't remember eating. Had I just been that dedicated to my work?

"Yup! I'm alive! I am *totally* alive!" I raised my hands in a pose like GLAY would do, but then realized that people might be staring and stopped.

"………"

I started to walk towards Kichijoji Station, but as I walked along by myself, in silence, I couldn't help but think about what had just happened.

Dr. Hashigami's list had 256 names on it, as if he'd predicted the 256 Incident. The names almost entirely matched the released list of victims.

My name had been on both lists. Why?

Were the people who died murdered, instead of committing suicide? Had Dr. Hashigami somehow found a list of people who were going to be killed? Was that why some evil organization had killed him?

If that was the case, then maybe they'd kill me, too. I still had the gold tooth key, for one thing.

"Wait, this is a *Mumuu*-style conspiracy theory! I've been watching too much anime!"

I was about to become the hero of a grand story, get caught up in a vast conspiracy, and go on a great adventure. Yeah. That was definitely what was about to happen. If that was the case, then I wanted a beautiful girl to travel with me! Maybe some hot, slutty older girl, or a younger girl with a giant rack and a really sharp tongue!

"Wait, what am I talking about?" I stopped in the middle of the road and looked around.

It was Saturday, so even though it was peak commute hour, there weren't that many students or salarymen around. It was a slightly warm, peaceful day in early spring. Everything felt shockingly normal.

But my heart was still pounding. It was like I'd been left behind as the rest of the world moved on.

"No, no, no. See? I'm touching this light pole!" I said, touching a light pole. "I can touch it! My hand's not going through it!" If I was dead, then how come I could touch a light pole?

Suddenly, I saw a Seimei High School uniform amidst the crowd. There was no school today. Was somebody going to school for a club activity?

A thought occurred to me.

How many days of school had I missed?

A single day might be ignored, but if I'd been absent for multiple days, I would've expected a call from the teacher.

"Did I…get any calls?"

Mom was busy at work, but if she heard I was skipping, she'd make time to come and tell me I needed to go to school. But I couldn't remember seeing her for the past several days…

Was I just spacing out? Or…

"Hmm…?"

As I tried to remember, I saw something fall from a girl's bag as she passed by me. I picked it up and saw that it was a pink pass case for the train. The train pass inside had the name "Saeko Kitaya" on it.

I instantly realized I'd made a mistake. Now that I'd picked it up, I had to call out to her and tell her she'd dropped it. But those kinds of communication skills were beyond me.

Sighing, I looked up to try to find her. But…

There were several women walking ahead of me, and I couldn't tell which one of them she was, even though I'd just seen her drop it.

Maybe I was more of a mess than I thought.

With perfect timing—or maybe awful timing, depending on how you looked at it—the crosswalk signal in front of me turned red. Everyone stopped to wait for the light to change. At this point, it would be worse for me if I didn't call out to her. People would think I took her pass case and walked off with it.

Sigh... I just wanted to get to Café Blue Moon.

I decided to work up my courage and talk to the woman in front of me, who was wearing a suit.

"U-um... e-e-excuse me!"

Crap... I sounded really creepy.

"Huh?" She turned around towards me, but quickly frowned and turned away.

Wow...totally ignored. That hurt. I mean, sure, I was creepy, but...

"U-um... did you drop your...pass case?" I said, my voice trembling, but she didn't even turn around.

At this distance, there was no way she couldn't have heard me. If she was completely ignoring me, that meant she must not have dropped it. In any case, there was no way I was giving it back after she was so rude!

Next, I talked to a girl who seemed to be in college and was wearing way too much makeup. She was playing with her smartphone while she waited for the light and looked like she was about to go on a date.

"U-um, did you drop your pass case?" This time I was able to speak normally.

"Huh? My pass case?" She began to rummage through her bag. Eventually, she pulled out a yellow pass case and frowned at me.

"It's right here."

"Oh, sorry."

Why'd she get so upset? I wasn't trying to hit on her. It took a lot of courage for me to talk to a girl I didn't know, and I was doing it out of the goodness of my heart, anyway. Man, girls are such a pain.

Maybe I should just assume whoever owned the pass case was long gone. Then I could just deliver it to the office at the station, and I wouldn't have to try any more of these draining conversations.

I saw a high school girl in a blazer waiting on the right for the light to change. I'd talk to her, and if that didn't work, I'd give up.

"U-um… S-S-Sa-Saeko K-Ki-Kitaya?"

"……?" The girl looked up at me when I said her name. She was a plain-looking, pigtailed girl who looked like a background character from an anime.

She stared at me suspiciously. Since she'd reacted, that meant she must be Saeko Kitaya. She only looked upset because a strange boy had called her name, and it wasn't because I was creepy… right?

"E-excuse me… you dropped your pass case…"

"Huh? Oh, that's mine!" She quickly took the case out of my hands. "Thank you so much!" She began to bow again and again. "I really appreciate it! I could've been in big trouble!"

"Oh, um, you're welcome."

She smiled and kept bowing. The light changed and everyone started to walk towards the station.

"I looked pretty cool just now, didn't I?"

Whoops. I was starting to grin. It wasn't often in my life that

I had a girl my age be grateful to me. "Yeah, she definitely has a thing for me. Maybe I'll get another Basara girl?"

If this really was a fated encounter, I'd see her again soon. She could graduate from being an extra and become a main character. Her looks were, well, average at best, but that meant that she could differentiate herself from Ryotasu and Myu-Pom. Put her together with Ryotasu, the weird one, and Myu-Pom, the popular one, and you could probably have a pretty good girl band.

Plus, there was one more thing I'd learned from my encounter with her.

"Dead people can't give back pass cases."

I felt stupid for being so scared a moment ago.

If I told Sarai about this, he'd laugh at me for sure. There wasn't a doubt in my mind that he'd laugh. It was just the kind of asshole thing he'd do. Not, of course, that I minded.

"It's great to be alive!"

It had been several days since I'd been to Café Blue Moon. I hadn't been here since the incident at Enmeiji. Actually, I'd never been here this early in the morning. I wasn't even sure they'd be open, but the sign said they were.

Would anybody come to a weird shop like this?

"Huh…?"

There was someone here.

It was still morning, but Ryotasu and Sarai were both inside the café.

Shouldn't they be at school? I'd been NEET-ing for a while, so maybe I wasn't one to talk.

"Oh, Gamotan! Samurai Gamonosuke! I was just about to call you!"

"Good timing."

"Wh-what's going on?" Ryotasu was one thing, but was I close enough to Sarai for him to wait for me?

I couldn't see Master Izumin at the counter. Maybe he was back in the kitchen.

Instead, there was a woman I didn't recognize at the counter. She was wearing a black suit, and her black hair was tied back in a ponytail. She wore stylish silver-rimmed glasses and gave off the aura of a capable businesswoman.

"Hello," she said.

"Oh... hi." I bowed, a little scared. She was staring at me like she was trying to figure me out, and I didn't like it.

Who was this woman?

Why was she staring at me like that?

"Wait, don't tell me..."

Was this the older sister of Saeko Kitaya, the plain-looking extra character whose pass case I'd just returned? They were both kind of plain-looking, so they had that in common! Maybe she'd come here to thank me for helping her sister!

Wait... no way. That would be like something out of a bad light novel. Besides, there was no way she could find me that fast.

"So, he's the boy?" the woman in the glasses asked Ryotasu.

"Yup! This is Samurai Gamonosuke!" Ryotasu puffed out her chest proudly.

"Huh? What?" Was this somebody who knew Ryotasu?

"Right, Gamotan?"

"Uh, right." I nodded. Ryotasu had introduced me to the woman in glasses, but I still didn't know what was going on.

The woman saw my confusion and handed me her card. "I'm sorry for bothering you like this. Here's my card."

I took it.

"What?!"

The card read: Monthly Mumuu *Editorial Department, Toko Sumikaze.*

"*Mumuu*? You mean *the Mumuu*?"

"I think it's the *Mumuu* you're thinking of, yes."

"Seriously?!"

Was this the woman who Myu-Pom was talking about? She'd said her name was Toko, after all, which matched the name on the card.

"Uhyaah…" I almost made a weird noise. No, I *did* make a weird noise.

This was my chance to meet an editor from the legendary occult magazine *Mumuu*! What an opportunity!

"U-um, what's someone from *Mumuu* doing here? Don't tell me you came to see me…"

"Yes, that's right. I heard about this place from Miyuu— I mean, Miss Aikawa."

Hell yes!

An interview from a magazine! If I got an interview with *Mumuu*, that would make Kirikiri Basara the prince of the occult world! There'd be no limit to how high my hit counter could go! There'd be no limit to how much I could make off affiliates!

"Maybe I'll be getting Ryotasu that ice cream sooner than I thought."

"Poyah?"

It felt like everything had been bad news lately, but finally the pendulum was starting to swing back! Maybe this was one of those monthly biorhythm things?

No, wait. Wait. I needed to stay focused here. We were about to talk business.

"A-ahem. If you're here to interview me about Kirikiri Basara, then can you tell me more about what we'll be discussing first? My site's a very scientific one, you see. It's about trying to shine a light on the mysteries of the world. I don't want to have a lot of amateurs flooding my site hoping to see scary pictures."

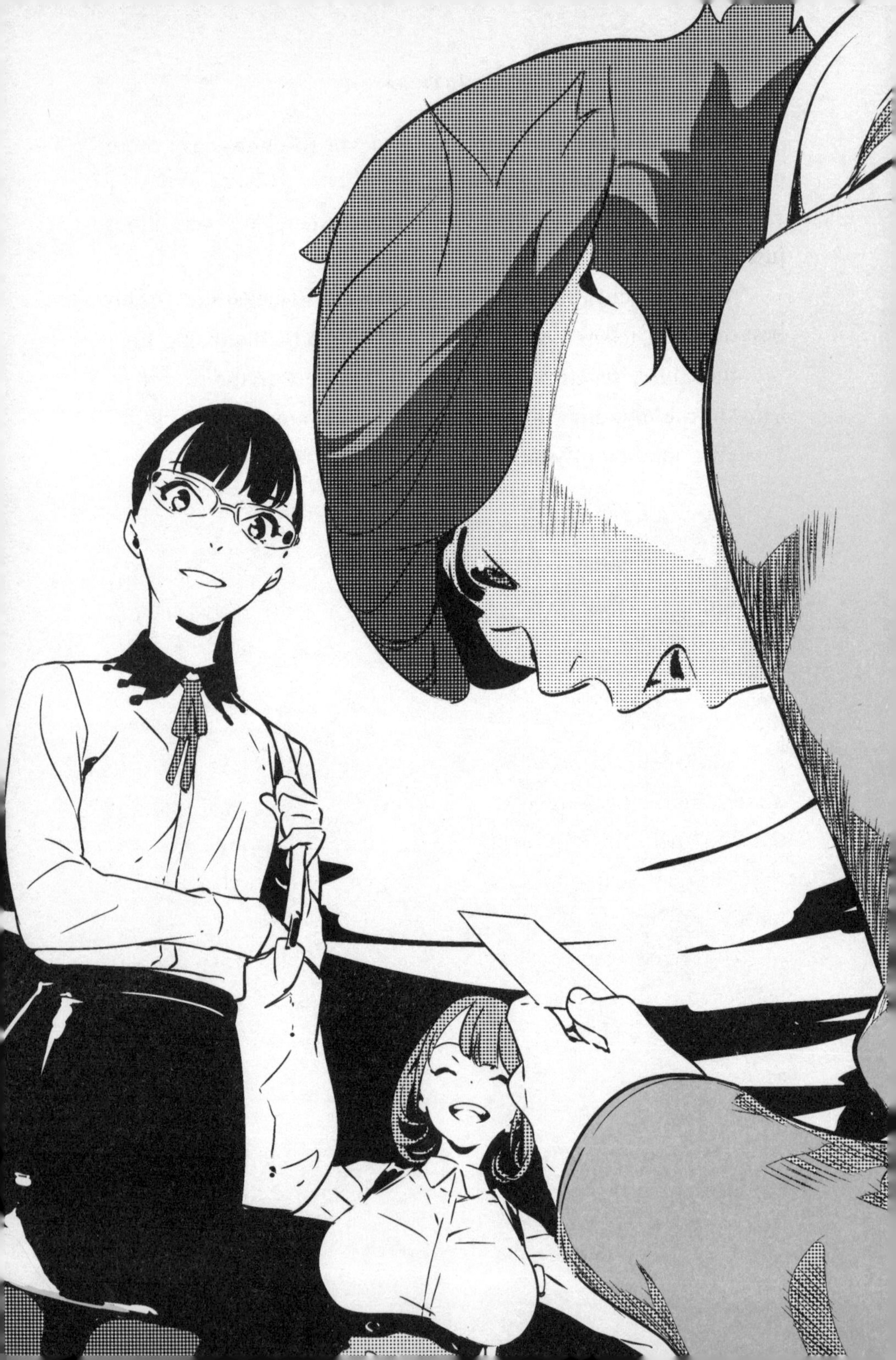

"Wah-wah! Gamotan! Gamotan! You're grinning! Grin, grin, grin, grin!" Ryotasu was pretending to be a cat and jumping around the room. Since I was having fun now too, I decided to just ignore her.

"Where would you like to begin?" I asked, "Maybe some of my best stories? Or how I get my information? Or perhaps—"

The editor for *Mumuu* chuckled. "Sorry, I'm not here for an interview. I came here to talk to you for personal reasons."

P-personal reasons? Did older girls have a thing for me? I mean, I was pretty average-looking, but lately a lot of younger girls had been into me. So this was a little surprising.

An older woman, huh? I'd never really considered the possibility, but the editor was cute, even if she was a little plain. I could see it working, especially since we likely had similar hobbies.

"Gamon, stop grinning. Miss Sumikaze is here to talk about the 256 Incident." Sarai's cold words brought me back to reality.

"She wants to talk to me about the 256 Incident?" I could understand if she wanted to talk about Dr. Hashigami, but why the 256 Incident? Maybe she wanted to get the opinion of the guy who ran Kirikiri Basara? But we weren't that well-known or important yet...

"Oh, right! Speaking of the 256 Incident, the weirdest thing happened." This was something I knew an editor from *Mumuu* would love to hear. "One of the victims had the exact same name as me. I couldn't believe it when I saw it."

"............"

"I never really thought about it, but maybe my name's a lot more common than I thought it was. It really had me scared for a second, though! Ahaha!"

I was laughing, but…

"Someone with the same name?" Sarai wasn't laughing. That wasn't unusual, but…

"That's right! The exact same name. It was enough to terrify even me. Even though I'm the admin of an occult blog, you know? Haha! Hahaha…huh?"

Why was the air suddenly so cold? And why wasn't everyone reacting like I thought they would?

I'd expected Sarai to look at me like I was an idiot, like he always did. But instead he was making eye contact with the *Mumuu* editor, Toko Sumikaze.

"Um…what's going on, guys?"

Toko's smile vanished as she spoke. "It might not be somebody else."

"…What?"

"You're not the only one. My name was on the list on the news, and so was Sarai's."

"Huh?" For a moment, I didn't understand what she was saying. Um…

It wasn't just me?

Toko was on the list, too? And so was Sarai?

"I'm sorry…what?"

I looked towards Sarai for help, and he nodded back. "Sorry. My name's not as common as yours."

How?

How could he just admit it like that?

I'd come to Blue Moon to talk to Ryotasu and Sarai so I could prove I was alive.

"Then that means you two are dead, too! That doesn't make

sense! Since when did you believe in the occult, Sarai?" I snapped at them.

I didn't regret it.

Paranormal Science NVL

Occultic;Nine

オカルティック・ナイン

There is no such thing as the "Occult." It can all be disproved by science.
Only those who have accepted everything
have the right to know the truth.

▶ site 54: Sarai Hashigami

"............"

Gamon sat down on the sofa in the café, clearly upset. Until a few minutes ago, he'd been screaming at me and calling me useless, but he'd finally calmed down.

"Fine, Sarai. I'll prove you're wrong. I'll show my real power as the admin of Kirikiri Basara. My real power!"

Now he was yelling at me. He was trying to sound strong, but I could see a thin film of sweat on his forehead.

He was probably worried.

So was I, but panicking here wouldn't help anything. This was precisely the time when one needed to be calm, collected, and capable of analyzing the situation thoroughly.

"Poor, poor Sarai-kyun!"

"........"

There was one girl in the room who was neither calm nor collected, instead dancing around the room singing a weird song. I wasn't sure if Ryoka Narusawa was actually trying to insult me or not, but the one thing I did know was that it was a waste of time to take her seriously.

I decided to start by talking about what I'd experienced since yesterday. I did this because the best move for now seemed to be sharing information with Gamon—or rather, Miss Sumikaze.

"The first thing that seemed strange to me was the way my mother reacted. I spoke to her, and she didn't say anything back."

"Y-you're sure it's not a coincidence? Your mom did seem to be pretty tired," Gamon answered quickly.

"Yes, but she couldn't have been *that* tired."

I'd screamed in her ear and stood right in front of her eyes, but she kept acting like I wasn't even there. That had never happened before.

"And then there was the TV broadcast."

This morning, there had been an announcement that they'd found more names of the victims in the Inokashira Park incident. One of the names was mine.

"When I heard my name, I thought it had to be some kind of mistake."

"That's the only explanation. Why didn't you call and find out for yourself? The Sarai I know would've done that without needing me to tell him."

"Of course I called and asked." I cut him off. My voice was a little rougher than I'd intended it to be. This wasn't good. If I lost control here, we'd get nowhere. "I called the TV station to see if the name on the list was accurate."

"A-and what did they say?"

"The name list is correct. There was no mistake... They

were insistent."

"........."

"But that doesn't prove I'm dead."

"What?" Gamon stared at me in shock. He didn't seem to understand what I was getting at.

"For now, I don't know if the TV station was right when they said there was no error." It was just a possibility. They could have been lying. "How much evidence do you think the person I called at the TV station actually had? They were probably just saying that because I was on the list. So the next likely possibility is that the list was in error. Perhaps the list contained the names of people who weren't actually victims."

TV stations made mistakes all the time. It wasn't implausible at all to think they might have the wrong names on a list of victims.

"And if that's true, there are two more possibilities. Either the police were wrong when they announced the names, or the TV station was wrong when they reported them."

This had happened recently enough that the papers didn't have the list of names yet. We could assume that the TV station was the only one that did. Of course, I'd have to start reading the evening paper to be sure.

"Poyah! Messed-up broadcast! Miss Japan!" Narusawa started dancing again. She sure was taking it easy.

"As near as I can tell, my name was broadcast on two stations. That means it's most likely that the mistake was on the police's side, so I decided to call the police."

"Wh-what did the police say?!"

"The answer was what you'd expect: the broadcast was correct."

"What...?" Gamon's shoulders slumped in dismay. *Let me finish*, I wanted to say.

"The identification was done by checking their possessions and having their families confirm, so there's no way it could be wrong. That's what the police said."

"S-so that's how they did it?"

"Don't jump to conclusions. It just means that one possibility has been ruled out. There's still a chance that any amount of human error could've taken place between the time the list got to the TV station and when it was broadcasted."

Only after investigating every one of them and ruling out the possibility of error could we be sure that both Gamon and I, as well as Miss Sumikaze, were actually among the victims of the 256 Incident. Even then, that would only mean the list was correct. It didn't necessarily mean that we were dead.

"Oh, wait! Wait a second!" Gamon gasped as if he'd suddenly had an idea, and grabbed on to me. "You said you called the TV station and the police, right? You talked to them over the phone? That means you were able to talk to them, right? What kind of ghost can talk on the phone?! Okay? Q.E.D.!" Gamon pumped his fists in the air. He swung between depression and excitement in an instant. It looked exhausting. "And when I was on my way here, I picked up this really cute girl's pass case. Her name was Saeko Kitaya! I was able to talk to her completely normally! You know what that means, right? It means I'm alive!"

"Saeko Kitaya..." I took out my phone and searched through a list of the people who'd committed suicide during the 256 Incident.

"W-wait, what are you looking at?"

"Saeko Kitaya... found it." The name was on the list. "That woman's name is among the 256 victims."

"What? But..." Gamon's eyes opened as wide as they possibly could, and then he froze. "But I... I just talked to her... she was really grateful. She said she dropped it all the time, and that she thought it was really hot the way I'd given it back to her..."

"It's possible you were only able to talk to her because she was dead, too."

"But she had legs! She wasn't floating! I couldn't see through her!"

He'd probably picked up his stereotypical idea of what a ghost looked like from watching old movies or something. I was about to tell him that, when...

"I actually did an experiment myself." Miss Sumikaze, who'd said nothing until now, began to speak calmly. "I tried to talk to several pedestrians at random. What I found was that, just like Gamon, I was able to talk to some of them. But—"

"Some of them you couldn't. In fact, most of them you couldn't. Right?"

"Yes."

I guess everyone had the same idea. I'd tried the same thing. I'd only been able to get a sample of twenty or so people, but in my case, I hadn't been able to talk to a single one.

"I was able to talk to two people. The odds that I'd run into two out of 256 people at random in Kichijoji are pretty low, so it's possible that we can talk to the living as well as the dead."

"Talk to the living?" I asked. "What would be the conditions for that?"

"Someone with a strong sixth sense, perhaps?"

"........."

What she was describing was the occult. There was no logic in that.

Toko Sumikaze.

She was an editor at the magazine where my dad's column used to run. Sometimes she would come to my house, but I couldn't remember ever speaking with her.

She seemed to be pretty quick on her feet, mentally, but just like you'd expect from an editor at *Mumuu*, she was the type who really believed in that stuff.

"Um, before we talk about people with a sixth sense, shouldn't we think about the possibility that they were just ignoring us?" Gamon said, desperately trying to come up with an excuse. "I mean, think about it. If you were walking down the street and somebody came up to you and said, 'Can you see me?' how would you react? I'd think they were with some kind of weird religious cult and ignore them."

"I thought about that, so instead I just asked for directions," Sumikaze responded.

"Uh…"

"I tried that with about fifty people, and only two of them reacted. The rest ignored me."

"W-well, you know. People in Kichijoji have gotten really rude lately…"

"That's an awful excuse. You know that, right?"

"Uh…"

Debating with him like this was a waste of time. If we couldn't remove our emotions from this, we'd never get anywhere.

I needed to tell myself this, too.

"Y-you seriously think you're dead because some people just ignored you? That's stupid! It's impossible!" Gamon ignored my warning—or no, maybe it was *because* of my warning—and became even more emotional. "I keep saying this, but we're talking to each other right now, right? And Sarai, you said you talked to the police and the TV stations on the phone, right?" he yelled. "And look, if I was dead I couldn't drink this tea!"

Gamon walked up to the counter and took a big gulp of iced tea from the glass there.

"Oh! That's the one I ordered!"

"Ryotasu, stop! We're talking about something important, so go dance over there!"

"Poyah?"

Gamon chased Narusawa away, then raised the glass so we could see it. "Let's say we're dead, and we don't actually have bodies. That means that this glass is just floating up on its own, tipping over, and then the tea is disappearing to who-knows-where! So, what, we're like poltergeists? And disappearing tea is a hell of a lot scarier than ghosts! It violates the laws of the universe!" he screamed. "The tea disappeared and the universe is in danger!"

Gamon rifled through the pockets of his duffel coat and pulled out a chocolate candy called Black Thunder. He ripped off the wrapper and took a big bite.

"Mmm! It's so good! This Black Thunder is so good! I can eat, not just drink!"

"Gamotan, Gamotan, give me a Black Thunder, too!" Ryotasu said.

"Too bad! I only had the one!"

"Poyah…" Narusawa looked depressed.

"I can even get on the internet from my smartphone! That alone is proof I'm alive!"

He was right. So we had circumstantial evidence that showed we were alive and we were dead.

I didn't want to think I was dead, either. That's why I had to disprove all the pieces of circumstantial evidence that showed I was dead, one at a time. The biggest piece of evidence right now was the list of suicides from the 256 Incident that had been broadcast on TV.

That, and the fact that we happened to have a list of several names that matched it. That was what had been bothering me the most.

"I—"

I thought for a moment about whether I should really talk to Gamon and Sumikaze about this. It felt to me like I might be getting too emotional. But I just couldn't shake the feeling that the hint was an important one.

It was a total conspiracy theory, but still…

"I think the encoded list my father left might have something to do with this."

"Huh? That list?" Gamon asked.

"I'm sorry, what list is this?"

I hadn't told Miss Sumikaze yet, had I?

I cut Gamon off before he could try to stammer out an explanation.

"I'll skip the details, but I have a list of encoded names my father gave me." The encoded message had been hidden on the ceiling of my dad's study. When we'd decoded it, we'd found 256 names. "Right now, more than fifty names match the list of suicides from the 256 Incident."

I'd asked Gamon to do the decoding. I nodded at him to tell me what he'd learned.

He hesitated for a moment before opening his mouth, as if he'd simply resigned himself to it. "I decoded seventy total. My name… was on the list."

So I was right. That meant my name was likely to be found, too. Did Dad…know this? Either way, it was even less likely to be a coincidence now.

"Ascension…!" When Miss Sumikaze heard this, she got so excited her cheeks flushed slightly. "Does this mean we might have been caught up in some kind of incredible conspiracy?"

I almost groaned. She was probably right. So she was a conspiracy theorist, too? I guess that was natural if she worked for *Mumuu*.

"A conspiracy? Honestly, I'd rather not agree with you." I barely managed to get the words out without my voice breaking.

"But there's no way 256 people just decided to kill themselves at once," she said. "Doesn't it make more sense to assume that someone is behind this?"

"My father knew who was behind it, and that's why he left the list. And the conspiracy killed him. Is that what you're trying to say?"

The words came out more smoothly than I'd expected. Probably because I'd been thinking the same thing. It was completely illogical, to the point where I almost hated myself for thinking it. But even so, I had to think it anyway.

It was, if nothing else, possible.

"Hey, Sarai. How many people know about Dr. Hashigami's list?"

"I only learned about it very recently myself. But it's clear that someone was looking for it. On the day my father was killed, someone ransacked the study in my house."

"Ascension... I had no idea." Miss Sumikaze shook her head a little in astonishment. "So at least we know whoever did that was real..."

"And we don't know who killed my father yet, either."

"They searched your house but didn't find the list, right? Does that mean they haven't found it yet?"

"There's no way to know for sure. We don't even know who did it."

Suddenly I saw an intensity in Miss Sumikaze's eyes, behind her glasses. She leaned forward.

"Sarai, Dr. Hashigami changed his opinion on the occult fairly recently, didn't he?"

"Huh? Y-yes, yes he did." I saw the resolution in her eyes and tensed up.

"He was never a believer in the occult," she said, "until he was. And that's when he started to try to get on television. Did you ever hear why?"

"No. But it was about five years ago when it became clear that he'd changed his mind. That was when my dad joined the SPR— the Society for Psychical Research."

That's when I'd started to despise him. I'd been so disappointed that a man who'd put so much emphasis on visible proof and who'd hated airy, poorly-developed theories had suddenly changed his mind.

"He once told me a theory that the soul normally lives within the brain, and when the heart stops, it's ejected outwards. Do you know about it?"

"Yes."

"The body is just a vessel for the soul. The soul is the most important organ, and when the body dies it becomes defenseless. Maybe that's the state we're in right now."

Suddenly Miss Sumikaze jumped topics.

I may have been the one to connect my dad and the 256 Incident, but that was far too much of a leap of logic for me. I tried to tell her this, but…

"W-wait!" Before I could, Gamon stood up and interrupted her. "Forget the conspiracy theory. If that's true, then you're saying we're ghosts, right? I still haven't accepted that!"

"Depending on your definition of 'ghost,' you could say that's right, or you could say it's wrong."

"Huh?"

"Dr. Hashigami treated the soul as memories stored in magnetic fields. There are two layers of protection for those memories. The first is electricity, and the second is the physical body. Like a Matryoshka doll."

This was bad news. Miss Sumikaze was totally fired up. Since she was my dad's editor, she knew all about his theories.

"Let's say that memories stored in these magnetic fields somehow left the body, and instead moved, for some reason, to become an electromagnetic field attached to the subatomic particles in the air. These particles would now contain our memories and personality from life. They would be our soul…" she said. "What if that's what happened to us?"

I need to tell her she's wrong, I thought. But for some reason, I couldn't.

My throat was so dry. I realized how dry it was and forced myself to gulp.

What she was saying was impossible. Normally I would've been able to tell her so, probably with a mocking look on my face. But... what was happening to us right now? Did I really have any evidence that could prove her wrong?

"No, I don't know..." Gamon seemed uncertain as well. "If we are these particles, then like I keep saying, how are we talking? How is a ghost supposed to do that?"

"I don't know that either..." Miss Sumikaze's shoulders slumped. "I guess all we have now is a theory that we were involved in some kind of conspiracy."

She didn't seem that attached to her theories. Or perhaps she wasn't a conspiracy theorist at all—simply an editor who was looking at things objectively. If that was the case, I'd feel very reassured.

"Sure, we don't have any proof we're dead," I said, "but we don't have any proof we're alive, either."

In the end, possibilities were just possibilities, and no amount of debate was going to prove anything.

"But we're, like, breathing right now!" Gamon seemed to have no intention whatsoever of admitting he was dead. He was getting angry and argumentative. "I'm speaking! I'm sitting in a chair! Can ghosts do that?"

They can. What would Gamon say if I told him that? Of course, I didn't intend to do so.

Over the course of my twenty-three-year life, I'd seen lots of things that weren't of this world. Most people would call it a sixth sense. When I'd brought it up a moment ago, Sarai had clearly looked upset, so I'd let the subject drop. But the reason I was still calm, compared to Gamon, was that my sixth sense had shown me all kinds of things over the years. In fact, the strange state we now found ourselves in wasn't that unusual to me.

"'The world you're seeing now is real. It's not a dream.' How do you think you could you prove that statement true?" Sarai asked me. It was a strangely philosophical question.

Dr. Hashigami had asked me that question once. What did I

say to him then? I couldn't remember clearly.

Gamon snorted. "That's easy. Just pinch your cheek."

Immediately, Narusawa grinned and demonstrated by pinching him hard on the cheek.

"Owww! That hurts, Ryotasu! No!"

"You're not dreaming, huh?" she said, smiling.

"Oh, right! That's right! See? Pain means it's not a dream."

Sarai sighed and shook his head. "What if it's a dream where you feel pain? This is no different than being uncertain if you're alive or dead. It's not something you can figure out on your own."

Huh? This feeling... Was Sarai starting to get emotional, too?

"Listen..." Gamon had been trying to force himself to be energetic and positive. Now he didn't try to hide his frustration at being shut down. "If you want to play that game, then you can't prove whether we're alive or dead regardless of the list."

Sarai didn't say anything. He was nervous, too. Who knew it was so hard to prove that you were alive? I'd lived my whole life without ever thinking about it.

"Okay! I vote we go with Sumikaze's conspiracy theory!" Gamon yelled.

"You know, just going with the theory you want to believe is the same as not thinking at all."

"So what, Sarai? You want to tell me that you're dead?"

"Of course not!"

"Then—"

Just as Sarai and Gamon were about to get into a fight, though...

"Hey, hey, Gamotan!"

Narusawa started to spin around Gamon in a circle. I was

too stunned to speak. It wasn't just me. Sarai and Gamon were both frozen, too. Oblivious, Narusawa danced around the café in a manner that was slow and relaxed, if not beautiful, before finally pointing a finger at Gamon.

"Now...now! Now is the chance for frozen yogurt!"

"Huh?" Even Gamon didn't seem to know what she meant.

"Your blog is a thing for turning weird stuff into frozen yogurt, right?"

"...?"

"Which means, Gamonosuke, that you need to write an article about this and try to earn me that frozen yogurt!"

Hmm? So that was it.

"Th-that's right...Kirikiri Basara!" Gamon figured out what she was saying at the exact same time I did. "We make this into a ridiculous article like the ones in *Mumuu*! It's so stupid that occult fans are sure to jump on it!"

Gamon excitedly grabbed his laptop off the table. "This might be the first livestreamed ghost experience in history! If we upload it in real-time like that thing with Kisaragi Station, it's a great chance to get some huge access numbers!"

"Kisaragi Station" was an urban legend about a fictional train stop; people sometimes saw it on social networking sites. It had originally gotten its start on 2channel. By uploading a series of messages in real time, which claimed to be from a man who'd gotten lost in a station that shouldn't exist, it led readers to believe it was a real story. At least, that was how it was supposed to work.

Since I worked at *Mumuu*, I knew all about it.

"If this works, I can finally make that affiliate money! Way to go, Ryotasu! You're really earning that Number One Basara Girl title!"

"Hee hee! I got a compliment! I did a great job!" Ryotasu started to spin around the café happily.

"So maybe the title should be 'I Suddenly Became a Ghost. AMA.' Or maybe, 'The NEET God Changed Classes Into a Ghost? LOL.' No, maybe something more straightforward, like 'I've Been Caught Up In the 256 Incident.'"

Gamon mumbled as he tapped away at his keyboard. He was working so hard on his article, it was like he'd forgotten we existed. "No, I need to think about this more," he went on. "There are lots of aggregator articles on this, so I need something that'll really stand out. I could attract a lot of trolls. They're everywhere."

"Trolls? Fee-fi-fo-fum?"

"No, maybe it would be better if there *were* trolls?"

Sarai watched him a bit before sighing a little. "Does he just have no idea how much danger he's in?"

"Maybe he doesn't want to think about it? I said a lot of things, but I basically feel the same way. If this is a dream, I want to wake up."

"That's just more reason to get a firm understanding of what's going on here."

It seemed like Sarai's personality was as serious as he seemed to be. For some reason, he seemed really young when I looked at him. It was strange, since I'd only been out of college a year myself.

I'd known Dr. Hashigami for a pretty long time, but I didn't know his son Sarai that well at all. This was probably our first real conversation, but for some reason, it didn't feel that way. Was it because Dr. Hashigami used to talk about his son a lot?

"My son's a smart boy, but he's very stubborn. A lack of flexibility is a flaw in a scientist."

I'd also heard that Sarai insisted the afterlife wasn't real and that he'd gotten into lots of fights with his father. That's why it was a little surprising to me that he'd brought up his dad at all.

"About what you were saying before... Dr. Hashigami's list. If you're looking into it, I'd like to help."

"Journalism?"

"That's part of it. I know it might not be appropriate, but..." Looking at Gamon had triggered my editor's soul. I chuckled and shrugged. "But in a way, I'm a part of this, too. I'm pretty close to both of these incidents. Dr. Hashigami did a lot for me. If he left this list because he wanted us to know something, I want to help in any way I can."

Sarai fell silent for a minute before adjusting his glasses with his fingers and turning to me. "The first thing we need to do is finish decoding the list he left for us. Then we need to match it to the list of the suicides from the 256 Incident and see if they really are related. If we learn something, I'll contact you."

"All right. Thanks."

What would the editor-in-chief say if I told him about this? He'd want to make a huge series about it in *Mumuu*. For Sarai's sake, though, it seemed better to avoid that. I had more pressing matters to deal with, anyway.

"By the way, Sarai, did you go see your corpse?" I wasn't sure if that phrasing made any sense, but there was no other way to put it.

Sarai's expression was as serious as ever as he shook his head. "No. Not yet."

Gamon, from the look of it, hadn't done so either.

"There can't be that many places you can store 256 corpses. Given the size of the case, we could probably find out by asking the police or city hall." Or maybe it had already been broadcast. If nothing else, the media should know.

Sarai didn't argue. Gamon seemed unlikely to help, so I gave up on him. From now on, Sarai and I would work together to try to get clear proof.

"I want to know as soon as possible if my corpse is there." That would be the fastest way to know if I really was dead. If I saw my own body, that would prove it. If I didn't, I couldn't be sure. "I know some people in the media I can ask. That is, if I can talk to them." I laughed a little, but Sarai nodded, expressionless.

If I *were* a ghost, come to think of it, then I would've died on the night of the 256 Incident, between February 29th and March 1st. Who had I talked to since then? I searched my memories and only came up with one name.

"Hey, Sarai, Gamon. You guys know Miyuu, right?" When she'd called me about the Kotoribako, I remembered her mentioning that these two were there. "What's she doing now?"

"I haven't seen her lately. She was in the hospital for a while, but I heard she left."

"Then she's back home?"

"Oh… That's right." Sarai gasped and covered his mouth with his hand. "We've talked with Aikawa a lot since March started. That means there's a chance she's dead, too…"

"I'll make time to go see her," I said.

Who else had I talked to, besides Miyuu? What about the

rest of *Mumuu*'s editorial department? I'd showed up at the office and talked to everyone the morning the incident had been on the news. We'd all watched it on the TV, and I'd talked to everyone… Actually, no; that conversation had been really strange.

Thinking back, had they heard me? Had they even seen me? I had to figure that out, too. I needed to figure out exactly who might be dead, and who might not be.

For now, I decided to call Miyuu.

PARANORMAL SCIENCE NVL

Occultic;Nine

オカルティック・ナイン

THERE IS NO SUCH THING AS THE "OCCULT." IT CAN ALL BE DISPROVED BY SCIENCE.
ONLY THOSE WHO HAVE ACCEPTED EVERYTHING
HAVE THE RIGHT TO KNOW THE TRUTH.

▶ site 56: Yuta Gamon

"It's no good. She's not picking up." Toko shook her head a little and put her phone back in her pocket. She'd called Myu-Pom, but she hadn't answered. It did seem like she was definitely able to make the call, though.

I'd watched carefully as Toko called Myu-Pom. The very fact that we could use phones was proof we weren't dead. There was no way a ghost could use a phone, right?

"I'm going to Miyuu's house," Toko said.

"Do you know where she lives?" Sarai had been clearly worried about Myu-Pom since her name had first come up. Maybe he was a secret Myu-Pom fan?

Was he after one of my Basara Girls? Maybe he just looked serious and was actually an asshole. That was the problem with college kids. Wait, what the hell was I thinking about?

"Do you want to come with me?" Toko asked.

"No," Sarai replied. "I don't have any reason to go."

The way he said it pissed me off, but at least Myu-Pom wasn't in danger anymore, so it was okay.

Toko ended the conversation and quickly left Blue Moon. I was worried about Myu-Pom as well. However, even if I went with Toko, I'd have no idea what to say to Myu-Pom. There was no way a NEET God like me could cheer up a teenage girl instead of just making her feel worse. If I had a list of choices like in an H-Game, maybe I could do it, but otherwise, no way.

As I sat there indecisively, Sarai stood up and put on his jacket, too.

"Y-you're leaving?"

"I need to know whether I'm dead or alive," he said.

"So you're going to look for your corpse? Wait…that sounds kinda cool. 'I'm going to look for my own corpse, baby.' Heheh. I'm using that in the article."

Sarai didn't respond.

He wanted solid proof no matter what. I guess that's what you'd expect from a science type. There was no way he'd find his own body, though. He was definitely alive.

"Gamon, I need you to finish decoding that list as fast as you can. I want to match it with the list of 256 Incident victims."

"Um, okay…"

God, he was so pushy. It wasn't like I was his slave.

I watched Sarai leave and then turned back to my laptop. The article was still in the outline stage. I needed to fill it with more things to attract a reader's attention.

"Proving whether you're alive or dead, huh?" I kept saying it, but there was no way we'd ever find our own corpses. My body was right here. If I confirmed that something wasn't there, was that proof I was alive? I decided to just turn my focus back to my article. I would start by gathering information I could use on the 256 Incident.

At least, that was the plan. When I searched Yahoo! News, I found information on the Enmeiji incident mixed in with articles on the 256 Incident. That article had a bunch of comments, too:

Murder Victim Stuffed into Box at Enmeiji; Victim Was High School Girl From Mitaka City

The police announced today that, after examining DNA evidence and the victim's belongings, the girl whose body was found partially stuffed inside a box on the grounds of Enmeiji temple was Chizu Kawabata, a resident of Mitaka city.

Kawabata had gone home from school with a friend on the 26th of the previous month, but went missing shortly after the two said goodbye.

The body was badly damaged, and the cause and time of death are both unknown. An autopsy revealed DNA belonging to someone other than Kawabata in the box, which the police are treating as an important clue.

There are also multiple witness reports from just after the box containing Kawabata was discovered, and the police are following those leads as well.

nat****
| What the fuck is going on in Kichijoji?!

oka****

Nobody's paying attention after the Inokashira Park incident, but the Kichijoji Urban Legends series is getting really nuts

kis****

I'm bored already. It's just a lame copycat trying to cash in on the fame. I get that there's this occult boom going on right now, but still...I hope the cops catch this guy soon.

sho****

I heard that there was human flesh inside that didn't belong to the girl, right? So does that mean there was more than one murder victim?

gou****

>>http://www.forestorage.co.jp/452axhhueayfenb49465/
Trigger Warning: GURO

ter****

You're shitting me. Where the hell did they get this photo?

yui****

I'm turning vegetarian.

kis****

It's a pretty good photoshop. Too real to be CG.

miv****

They still haven't caught the guy who did it? There's even witnesses. The Musashino cops are useless, lol

oji****

> The cops have been useless in general lately. Maybe they just don't care?

for****

> They do their best at issuing parking tickets. They've got quotas to meet.

sha****

> Speaking of car stuff, the taxies in front of the station are dicks. If you want to go a short distance, they just slam the door on you. How the hell am I supposed to get home when there's no bus?

ril****

> Walk, idiot. That place is always jammed because so many people park in the street.

soe****

> Sometimes I see cars with no drivers in them. They just leave the engine running while they go to the bathroom or something?

kur****

> Maybe they're ghosts.

hwl****

> I heard there's someone in Kichijoji who casts curses. Maybe they did it?

bob****

> They only do Western stuff. The Kotoribako is a Japanese thing.

quo****

| I thought it was Chinese?

man****

| Let's go to the sea brother. You love the sea.

ara****

| Nah, it's a Japanese curse. On the mainland they do their ethnic
| cleansing by killing the men. Killing the women so your enemies
| can't breed is a Japanese idea.

zas****

| It may be Western, but it's a Japanese girl running it lol

After seeing that box and hearing Myu-Pom's awful scream, I found myself hoping that every one of these commenters died. Then again, as administrator of Kirikiri Basara, there were probably a bunch of people on the internet who thought the same about me.

"It ain't easy being a NEET God…"

Neither the article nor the comments said anything about the boy I'd seen at Enmeiji. That strange, pale-white, almost inhuman boy.

He had to be the killer.

The cops were probably looking for him as hard as they could, but there was no news of him being arrested. I hoped somebody caught him soon.

He'd kept saying that as a minor he wouldn't be arrested, but there was no way that was true. There were laws for minors that would punish him. There had to be. If that happened, would Myu-Pom cheer up?

I shook my head and drove thoughts of Enmeiji out of my mind.

There was nothing I could do about it. For now, I would focus on writing the article on the 256 Incident. If I shared information with everyone, maybe I'd get a hint from somewhere unexpected. It was a bad idea to underestimate the information-gathering capabilities of an affiliate blogger.

"But you know, every aggregator's talking about the 256 Incident right now."

I had to laugh when I saw that even the game and anime sites were talking about it. What the hell did this have to do with games and anime?

But in terms of page views, they were monsters. They could spread things far faster than I could. Information was only good when it was fresh. After a while, it stopped being fresh, and thus, it stopped being valuable.

And while the 256 Incident might've been the top story right now, with a bunch of articles all saying the same thing, readers would be dispersed over several sites. It was already what they called a "red ocean." If I wanted to stand out amid that chaos, I needed something seriously sensational.

The thing with the 256 Incident, though, was that the only information available was the update with the victims' names. The TV was doing the usual crap where they interviewed each victim's family and talked about how sad everyone was.

"So maybe I need to do a live commentary...? It's gonna be one step below doxxing myself, so it does seem a bit dangerous."

Or could I maybe "interview" Sarai or Toko? Sarai was the son of Dr. Hashigami, and Toko was an editor at *Mumuu*. Either one could get me some serious page views.

"They'd probably get mad at me later, though."

Myu-Pom was out of the question. She was already in bad shape. If I did something to take advantage of her, she'd really start to hate me, and she might even sue me. My conscience wouldn't allow that, anyway.

"If only Ryotasu were dead... She's cute, and she's got those melons. And she's so stupid that I don't think she'd sue me," I whispered, and then felt disgusted at what an asshole I was.

This was no good. I was getting too close to the theme of "death."

"What? What's this about melons?" Ryotasu came up to me, sipping one of Master Izumin's nasty, nasty drinks.

Don't tell me she heard what I'd said to myself? If this were a light novel, maybe she'd have some strange power that let her read the text on the page.

"I-It's nothing."

"What? Don't hide things from me, Samurai Gamonosuke! Before you start eating melons, give me my frozen yogurt!" Ryotasu started to bounce up and down like a child throwing a tantrum.

"Th-the melons are swaying..."

"Po-yah? Oh, so that's what you meant by 'my melons'." She caught me staring and figured out exactly what I'd meant.

"N-no, that's not it..."

"Gamotan, you're a pervert!" Ryotasu grinned and pulled out the Poyaya Gun.

"W-wait! Time out! Time out!"

"I-shi-shu!"

"Ugyaaah!" A surge of electricity raced through my body as I screamed in pain.

Ryotasu looked at me, satisfied, and said, "Gamotan, sit there and think about what a naughty boy you are." And then she danced out of the café.

"Hey! …I can't believe she just left me here."

Even if she was mad, that was a dick move. At the bare minimum, she could've tried to make me feel better after hurting me with the Poyaya Gun.

"You okay, Gamotan? Want me to treat you to a delicious drink? Hehe!" Master Izumin had come back at some point. Until now, he'd been in the kitchen behind the counter.

"Don't worry about me."

I wanted someone to worry about me, but that someone definitely wasn't him. Now I didn't even feel like writing my article.

"Hey, Master Izumin… you can see me, right? You can hear me?"

"Oh, you mean what you guys were talking about? Of course I can see you, and hear you, too!"

"R-right? I'm alive, right?"

"How does a dead person drink something?"

"Right?"

"I was listening to you guys, and you were getting excited over the dumbest stuff. Listen. If you ask me, ghosts are something scary. Nothing more, and nothing less. You guys are just talking. You're not scary at all. You don't have any right to call yourselves ghosts, hehe!"

"That's Master Izumin for you! The thought processes of a twelve-year-old girl! But I like it anyway!"

The world was nice and simple that way. He was right. I wasn't dead.

I decided to take a walk to think more about what I'd do with Kirikiri Basara.

"And thus, the ghost went out for a walk… Master, put it on my tab! Actually, just give it to me for free! Ghosts can't make money!"

"It must be nice to be able to be a ghost whenever it's convenient for you, huh?" Master blew me a kiss as I left.

It was creepy. If I could find something creepy, that meant I wasn't dead.

▶ site 57: Shun Moritsuka

It was Saturday, and the open area in front of Akihabara station was filled with shoppers. Lately, it was common to see non-Japanese buying huge amounts of appliances and general household items. Japanese products were cheap, reliable, and if you were foreign, you didn't have to pay taxes.

After World War II, Akihabara had filled up with shops selling circuits, condensers, and other electronic parts. When the economy started to grow, it developed fast. In addition to customers looking for normal appliances, there were places to buy radios, audio equipment, and remote-controlled toys. People came from all over Japan to buy things.

When electronic games started to appear, the city moved from selling hardware to software. Now it was a mecca for otaku culture, and there was very little left to remind anyone of the time when it was called "the Electric City."

"Well, if this were a timeline where Faris-tan didn't exist, then maybe it would still be selling electronics. If this were *Steins;Gate*, that is." I grinned, thinking about the anime.

I looked around and saw signs everywhere covered with cute girls, hot boys, and lots of strange characters I didn't understand. The giant TV on the UDX played anime videos all day long. Akihabara was like a 3D website, in a way—a portal site to otaku culture.

There were no windows on the buildings, and all of them were covered with ads, some of which were put up and taken down in the course of a single night. It really was just like a website.

"I love the chaos here. Or I would, if it weren't for work. This is the best place to find good *Vanguard* cards, for one thing." But as a place for the action and drama-filled life of a detective, it was somewhat lacking. "There's no Castle of Cagliostro here."

It wasn't exactly good for hard-boiled noir stuff, either. There were rows of neon signs along the main drag. If they were only a little brighter and more obnoxious, it could give the place some atmosphere. But that was more of a Shinjuku or Kabukicho kind of thing.

The fact of the matter was that the place had become too famous overseas, and now it had changed to become more normal and touristy. Because of that, the unique sense of chaos and danger that the city offered was, compared to a place like Shinjuku, nowhere to be found—or if that was going too far, at least there was less of it.

In the past, there had been an atrocity here that had shaken the city to its foundation. But it had been sudden and random, with no politics and no conspiracies involved. In the end, all it left behind was a feeling of empty frustration.

I would never forget it. I wanted the person who ruined

everyone's treasured memories to spend the rest of their life in jail.

Crime didn't suit this town. That much was clear.

"But the whole 'underground' thing is gone now, too…"

Twenty years ago, there were tons of shady junk parts shops, as well as lots of suspicious-looking foreigners selling things down side alleys, I'd been told. But at this point, most of those had been cleaned out.

That must be why there weren't a lot of TV crime shows set in Akihabara. There was the occasional police car or uniformed officer, but they usually dealt with shoplifters or handling traffic. That was an important job too, but…

Some places had an atmosphere that suggested a dark and dangerous world, that inspired an almost instinctual fear. One could still sense that atmosphere in Kabukicho, but in twenty-first-century Japan, it was gradually disappearing from the cities.

It wasn't just Akihabara. Center Street in Shibuya and Ikebukuro Nishiguchi were a lot more peaceful than they used to be.

"I guess that goes for Kichijoji, too."

Kichijoji was one of the areas under the jurisdiction of my station, the Musashino Police. One could head down the back alleys there and only get a mild sense that something strange might be going on.

Sometimes there would be minor incidents, but never any crimes. Even Harmonica Alley, the area near the station, was a lot safer than it was a few years ago. It was no longer an underground black market, but a spot with a lot of yummy hidden restaurants.

The people on the streets were always kind and cheerful. On

the weekends, there were families and couples going shopping and relaxing at any number of different stores and cafés. It was a wonderful place to have a good time.

There was a reason it always ranked first place in surveys of "Towns in Tokyo You'd Want to Live in." It was a place the average person wanted to visit, and there were always lots of visitors from outside the city. Unlike Akihabara, there were a lot of old historical sites, like shrines. Stuff like that gave the locals a strange sense of peace. Maybe the temples protected the town with some kind of barrier that brought peace to the hearts of visitors?

Okay, that was just being silly. But that image of a cool, wonderful city had only lasted until a week ago.

A famous professor who'd been on TV was murdered in his lab at his college. Then 256 bodies, victims of a mass suicide by drowning, had been pulled up from the heart of Inokashira Park, the symbol of Kichijoji.

Ever since these two cases were reported, I'd seen fewer people traveling about the city, and no more lines at popular cafés and food stalls.

"Our station's been in an uproar, too."

We hadn't ID'd all the bodies yet. The problem was that, weirdly, over half the victims were carrying nothing that would identify them. Because of this, we detectives were being sent around to help identify the bodies. Despite the fact that everyone was busy, here I was wandering around Akihabara. If my co-workers Kozaki and Shinoyama saw me here, I'd be in for one hell of a lecture.

"Well, they won't be yelling at me when they see me anymore, probably."

I stood on the pedestrian bridge that connected to UDX, leaning up against the rails and looking down at the people below.

As I did, I thought about Shinoyama and Kozaki. I didn't know if we had different values or they just didn't like me, but those two had a habit of behaving really nastily towards me. Somehow, I felt a little sad when I realized I'd never be hearing their yelling again.

I thought back to what had happened just a few hours ago. I'd finished my morning work and come back to the station. Something had felt weird. The air was heavy, like it was hard to breathe. When I went to the floor where the detectives' division was, it got worse.

Part of my trouble breathing might just have been that I'd run up four flights of stairs, though.

"*Pant...pant...pant...* Man, I've got the worst luck. I just get back, and the elevator is getting repaired. My heart's pounding like a drum! Maybe I'm just getting old," I'd said, pretending to catch my breath even though I wasn't exhausted at all. To tell the truth, four flights of stairs was nothing. Compared to the way Inspector Zenigata ran from the bottom floor of the castle all the way to the top, this was nothing at all.

None of the other detectives had reacted to my joke.

"...?"

Sure, normally they'd just look at me coldly or get annoyed, but today there wasn't even that much of a reaction. Only silence. I could see the staff and investigators scattered across the room, but nobody said anything. They just kept at their work. This was the first time they'd completely and totally ignored me.

"What's wrong? Has there been some new development in the Inokashira case?"

Nobody answered.

"Hmm? Hello? Can you hear me?" I said to someone nearby, but there was no response. Not even the slightest twitch. Everybody was ignoring me completely.

That was strange… I'd worked pretty hard to establish a position as the guy in the department whom everybody beat up on. Maybe it was just my imagination, but everyone seemed really tense.

There was a strange air that hung over the whole floor. I decided to take the hint and stop messing around. "Did something happen?" I asked. No answer. Nobody even looked at me.

"Oh, dear." I tried waving my hand in front of one of my co-workers' faces, but I got ignored. Then I tried talking to someone sitting a bit away, but he didn't even look up at me.

What was going on here? Had I done something to make them hate me this much? I mean sure, sometimes I would blow off investigations to go hit up card shops. But I'd done my job as a detective—or at least I'd thought I had.

"Oh!"

Just then, Shinoyama and Kozaki came up the stairs, back from their investigation. As usual, the two of them were working together. At this point, I was willing to take even their sarcasm.

I walked over to them desperately. "Hey, listen to me, Shinoyama! Everybody's being mean to me!"

"I'm so tired… How come the elevator's being repaired?"

"You've got that right."

"What do you want for lunch, Kozaki?"

"I'm not hungry."

"Oh, I'm hungry," I said, raising my hand. "Want to go

somewhere?" This was perfect. I'd just found a restaurant with really good prices, and I'd been meaning to go back. "I just found this great place near here a week ago. The food is great, but it's in an out-of-the-way place, so it doesn't get crowded at lunch."

Even better, they didn't even care if you had an after-lunch cigarette, which was unusual for lunch places. Both Kozaki and Shinoyama were heavy smokers, so it was perfect for them. I didn't like cigarette smoke, so I'd always avoided going to lunch with them, but on a day like this I was willing to ignore it.

"I recommend the motsunabe stew," I said. "Although it's gotten a little warmer lately, so you might break into a sweat. And also—"

"I guess I can skip lunch today."

"Yeah, sorry."

"Huh? Um, excuse me?!" I spread out my hands wide and yelled, but they just slowly walked right past me. "Come on, now."

Even these two were ignoring me? *That's going a little too far.*

Just then, I finally realized they weren't wearing their beat-up old suits, but dark, black ones. Their neckties were black too, which meant...

"Why are you guys in mourning clothes?"

They didn't answer.

"Did you just get back from somebody's funeral?"

They didn't even look at me.

"Listen. I don't know what you're so mad about, but—"

They couldn't hear me.

"That bastard, making us do all this crap..." Kozaki took off his jacket and slammed it down on the back of his chair. For some reason, he looked so frustrated—and he was crying. Shinoyama was quiet; he didn't blame or agree with him. He just looked down with a serious expression on his face.

The two of them were clearly different than usual. What was going on here? And why were both of them glaring at my seat at my desk? It was almost like...

"Huh?"

Suddenly, intuitively, I realized.

A certain possibility came to my mind. It was just a possibility, but if I assumed it was true, everything made sense. Not like that made it any better. More than anything, it was so crazy that even I couldn't believe it.

"Um, I'm gonna go do some questioning," I said softly, then fled the station to clear my head.

Of course, nobody responded.

"And I was right." I took a sip from my warm canned coffee as I stared at the giant UDX screen from atop the overpass.

I'd tried several ways to see if my hypothesis was right. First, I went to my usual spot at the trading card corner at Gamers. Then to the café restaurant Backstage Pass, where I was basically a regular. Then the Sega arcade. I tried them all, and they all came back with the same, unshakable result.

To be honest, I was surprised. But strangely, I didn't feel angry or sad. If I did feel anything, it was...disappointment. "It" had happened, and for a while, I hadn't even noticed. I was disappointed by my own stupidity.

"Man, what a screw-up. I can't believe I'm dead. So I guess that means I only weigh twenty-one grams?" In 1970, the American doctor Duncan MacDougall had announced he'd proved a soul weighed twenty-one grams. I guess that meant I'd lost a lot of weight.

I sighed, tasting a bitterness that felt like defeat. Nearby, a group of otaku were leaning up against the railings just like I was and sharing what they'd bought with each other. I watched them out of the corner of my eye as I tried to decide what I needed to do next.

I was still in a bit of a state of shock, reasonably enough. Not only did I not have any kind of plan at all, my head was completely blank.

With nothing else to do, I decided to take my mind off it by looking at the giant UDX TV. The text on the screen read "More Victims in Inokashira Mass Suicide Case Announced," with a list of names scrolling down. I'd looked a moment ago, and sure enough, my name was there.

"Sheesh…" I'd come all the way to Akihabara because I wanted to shut the case out of my mind, but there was probably no way to do that in Tokyo right now.

The announcer on the huge screen was reading from the list of names, oblivious to my problems. They were already announcing the list of people who'd been identified today. Yuta Gamon's name was on the list, too. It was possible they'd ID'd over two hundred people now.

"In the end, I guess I couldn't stop it."

I'd just been forced to watch as their plan went forward. I thought of how stupid I'd been and tore at my hair.

"They forced me to dance with Nikola Tesla's ghost, and I never even realized it. I guess I'm just too old for this."

PARANORMAL SCIENCE NVL
Occultic;Nine
オカルティック・ナイン

THERE IS NO SUCH THING AS THE "OCCULT." IT CAN ALL BE DISPROVED BY SCIENCE.
ONLY THOSE WHO HAVE ACCEPTED EVERYTHING
HAVE THE RIGHT TO KNOW THE TRUTH.

A few days ago, our graduation ceremony was postponed.

I only found out the day of the ceremony, and I hadn't been happy about it at all, but neither I nor any of the other graduating seniors were surprised. At least, none of the students or their parents said anything. Of course, somebody might have complained privately. Honestly, if they'd gone ahead with the ceremony anyway despite what was going on, I probably would have wondered if the school had gone insane.

The school never really announced the reason for the postponement, but we all knew. I went to Seimei High. We were on the same grounds as Seimei University, where a famous professor had been killed last month. His killer still hadn't been caught. And then there was the suicide of 256 people in Kichijoji's famous Inokashira Lake. After those two incidents, there was no way the school would hold a graduation ceremony.

It was still morning, but the atmosphere in class 3-A was relaxed.

"Hey, what are we gonna do after this?"

"There's time. Let's go somewhere."

"I can't. My parents say I'm absolutely not allowed to stop anywhere."

"Gotcha. Yeah, it's been dangerous lately."

"They're too worried. It's seriously annoying."

I could hear my classmates saying things like that around me. It was a Saturday, but there was a meeting to explain the graduation postponement, and we third-years had all been forced to come to school.

We were told that it was postponed, not canceled, but they were still working on the date. Of course, I thought that if that were the case, they could've just waited to hold the meeting until they had picked a new date, but after that we were all sent to homeroom, which was quickly over.

Since school ended at a weird time, a lot of my classmates were talking about afternoon plans. Those kids who had plans or who hadn't finished their college exams yet left immediately after homeroom. I should have done the same thing, but during the long explanation at the meeting, I'd started to feel a little sick. I'd decided to rest a little until I felt better, and missed my chance.

I took a quick glance out the window. It was Saturday, so the first- and second-year students weren't here. The schoolyard was empty, and there was nobody out at the stadium, either. It felt kinda weird. A month ago, I never would have imagined putting on my uniform and coming to school at this time.

March was a busy time for third-year students. For those who had already decided their post-graduation plans, it was the time to prepare for a new life. Some of those people were leaving home and going all alone to a place they'd never been. But there were also people who hadn't finished their exams. There were even some people who hadn't passed their tests or found a job and were too stunned to do anything.

What about me?

Where did I—Asuna Kizaki—fall among those people?

"Hey, did you hear? Some of our school's students were on the list of Inokashira suicides."

"Seriously? Who? Someone in our grade?"

"A boy in second year. He hadn't been to school in a long time."

"You sure he isn't just absent?"

"The rumor says that nobody's seen him since the day it happened."

"Sure it was a boy in second year? I heard it was a girl in first year."

"First year? You know her name?"

"Um… you know, the girl who was doing fortune-telling on Nico?"

"Huh? Seriously? I've seen her! You're kidding me!"

Several boys were talking loudly in the seats behind me.

The group suicides…

It was definitely a sensational event.

There had been days of reporting on it, but there were still many mysteries. It was the perfect topic for rumors, especially since it had happened right next to our school. I'd deliberately avoided hearing anything about the incident, so I didn't know the details, just that 256 people had killed themselves in a single night.

I should just stop getting involved in this stuff.

When I'd left America and moved to Japan a year or so ago, that had been my decision. I wanted as peaceful a life as I could get, a quiet one where I didn't make any waves. Otherwise, I'd just shorten my own lifespan.

"Don't try to turn off your ears. Turn off your mind. Just ignore them."

I remembered the words of the person who'd taught me that, and blanked out my mind. That helped shut out the conversations around me.

I was feeling a little better, so it was time to go home. I took my phone out from my backpack. I was terrible with smartphones, maybe because I always wore black gloves. Phones always felt like they were going to slip out of my hands. With some difficulty, I was able to turn on the phone's screen and display the time. There were just a few minutes until noon. I had an appointment at the hospital after this, but first I needed to get lunch somewhere. I stood up to go.

"Kizaki." Suddenly I heard my name from behind me and turned around. One of my classmates, a girl with her hair in long braids, was standing there.

What was her name again? How could I not know this when I'd spent a year in the same class as her? When you spend your days doing nothing, it's easy to forget names. But it would be rude to ask now. Once we graduated, there would be nothing connecting us at all.

"Kizaki, you're done with exams, right?" The girl with the braids smiled, looking a little embarrassed.

"Yeah, I'm going to Seimei University."

You could go to Seimei University from Seimei High, of

course, but it wasn't an automatic thing. They took your grades and attendance into account. There was a test, too, but it wasn't that hard. Until a year ago, I'd lived in America, and I wasn't used to Japanese tests at all, but I was still able to pass.

"Oh, I thought so." The girl with the braids sighed with relief. "Listen, are you busy today? All the girls who are going to Seimei are going to go to karaoke."

"Karaoke?"

"Yeah. We were hoping you could come, too… How about it?"

She seemed really hopeful. It was the first time in the past year someone at this school had shown me this much kindness, so I hesitated. But when I saw the three girls who were standing behind her—they were classmates too, but I couldn't remember their names at all—I instantly understood what was going on. They were all staring at me, not bothering to hide their irritation. They must've been the "girls who were going to Seimei."

I ran my tongue along my lips to wet them, then deliberately dropped my phone, taking care not to make it look unnatural.

"Oh!" The girl with the braids look surprised and quickly crouched down to pick it up.

When she was distracted, I took off my gloves. "I'm sorry, I was being careless…"

I apologized and pretended to pick up my phone. When I did, I touched my finger against the back of her hand. Then I closed my eyes.

Begin the performance.

A blackness spread across my vision. As I dove deeper and deeper into my mind, I began to see a wooden door. I slowly opened it with an invisible hand, only to be confronted with a series of doors in different colors. They spread out endlessly, one after another. All the doors were already open, and I went through one after another like I was going through a series of torii arches on the way to a shrine. Deeper and deeper I went. When I got to the door at the far bottom, a white cat jumped up. Our eyes met, and I peered deep into its eyes.

The next thing I knew I was in a small movie theater, sitting in one of the seats. I was the only person in the audience. The projector began to move on its own, and a grainy, worn-out image appeared on the screen.

It was the memories of what I'd touched. It didn't matter if it was a person or a thing; it always started with the newest memories and moved backwards, going through all the most important "scenes" one after another.

Psychometry.

The power to read someone's—or something's—memories by touching it.

"What? You're inviting Kizaki, too? Why?"

On the screen, I saw not the girl with the braids, but one of the three who'd been watching me from behind her. This was the girl with the braids' memory, and I was seeing it through her eyes, so all her friends were smiling gently. It was totally different from the looks they'd given me.

"Yumi, are you friends with Kizaki? I've never seen her talking to anybody. Isn't she…kind of scary?"

"Scary? I don't know. I've never talked to her, either."

So the girl with the braids was named Yumi. She was right. I couldn't remember talking to her, either.

"So why invite her?"

"The teacher said she's going to Seimei, too. Once we change schools, we'll have no way of getting in touch, right? So I wanted to at least have a way to contact her."

"Why? What would you ever say to her?"

"Huh…? Is it wrong to ask?"

"Sigh… do what you want, then. It's going to make things less fun for me, though."

On the screen, all of Yumi's friends were sighing. I stood up and closed the curtains on the screen.

Performance complete.

I opened my eyes, and I was back in the classroom. The performance had only lasted for an instant. I'd recorded a video of myself using psychometry once, and even the longest ones had only lasted three seconds.

Yumi was still kneeling in front of me. She offered me my phone. "Here. The screen's not cracked."

"Thanks. I'm sorry." There was a double meaning in my apology as I took the phone and stood up.

Her friends were watching me silently. They still looked upset.

"Don't worry." I smiled at them, and their eyes all went wide at once. They all looked away from me awkwardly. I turned back to Yumi. "I appreciate the invitation, but I have to go to the hospital."

"Huh? The hospital? Are you sick?"

"A little, maybe. I can't keep the doctor waiting, so I'm going to get going."

"Yeah, sorry for inviting you so suddenly."

"Goodbye," I said, and then I left the room.

As I walked down the hallway, Yumi's face began to disappear from my memory. Maybe I should have at least gotten her last name, but my memory was already over capacity, and I had gotten into the habit of quickly deleting any information I didn't need.

I went out into the schoolyard and looked back up at the building. I'd transferred into this school last spring. I'd spent a year coming here almost every day. In the end, I'd never managed to fit in. Of course, that was only natural, considering I'd never really tried.

No matter what you hid behind the words you spoke, my psychometry could see through it. There was no doubting that because of this, my personality was a bit colder than the other girls in my class—for example, Yumi, the girl who'd just talked to me.

I knew I didn't look down on the people around me, but that was probably how the others interpreted it. For one thing, my health often meant I came to school in the afternoon or left before the day was over. As a rule, I never participated in gym class. I didn't participate in most school activities, including the school fair. If I went at all, I just sat on the side and watched. Of course there was no way I was going to fit in.

Maybe I didn't need to force myself to go to the graduation ceremony… It would be rough on my health for me to come all the way back to the school.

"Goodbye," I said to no one in particular, and left.

I was being followed. I'd started to sense it on my way toward Kichijoji Station after going to the hospital. I'd done work in the past that would justify someone tailing me, and I'd been trained to know how to deal with it. But ever since I'd come back to Japan, nothing like that had been a part of my life. It was a bigger surprise than I thought it would be.

More than anything, I was confused. Right now, I was just a student. What was the point of following me now? I couldn't understand what they would want. Or was it the killer from the murder at the college? I had nothing to do with the murdered professor, but there was a chance the killer had settled on a lone teenage girl walking through the streets as his victim. The thing was, the way they were following me didn't feel like they were an amateur.

Just then, my chest started to clench up hard. I couldn't breathe at all from the pain. A sensation of numbness ran through my whole body. I bit down hard on my lip to keep from passing out.

I couldn't slow down. I couldn't let my pursuer know what had happened. I put my right hand on my chest, pressed down, and took a series of short, deep breaths to quell the pain.

Calm down, I said to myself as I headed away from the path to the station and into the narrow alleyways.

From the big streets to the small ones. From the residential areas to the back alleys. Over the course of the last year, I'd pounded the details of this area's geography into my head. It was an old habit. Kichijoji was a town with lots of tiny houses clustered together and many small paths and narrow spaces. There were telephone wires strung above my head and lots of poles along the street to support them.

I went deeper into the narrow alleyways. The pursuer was no

longer trying to hide their footsteps and was following me quickly. I listened for the footsteps, walking until I found a house with a wall the height I was looking for. When I turned a corner and left my pursuer's sight, I quickly climbed up the wall. I leapt from there to one of the telephone poles. There was no time to think about the fact that my skirt was flying up.

My pursuer seemed to panic after losing me in the narrow, complex alleys. They stopped trying to hide themselves at all and began to run. They ran right past me without realizing I was there. As soon as they were in front of me, I jumped down.

"Freeze!" I said in English, using a low, threatening voice. I pressed myself up against their back and wrapped an arm around them, pushing a ballpoint pen into their neck. It may have been just a pen, but it could easily tear through the carotid artery. They must've known it too, because they didn't resist.

Once I was pressed up against them, I was able to get a better idea of who they were. They were male, and quite tall. I felt like a little kid pressed against a grown-up. His body was well-muscled enough that I could tell even through his coat. He didn't have the frame of a Japanese person, either.

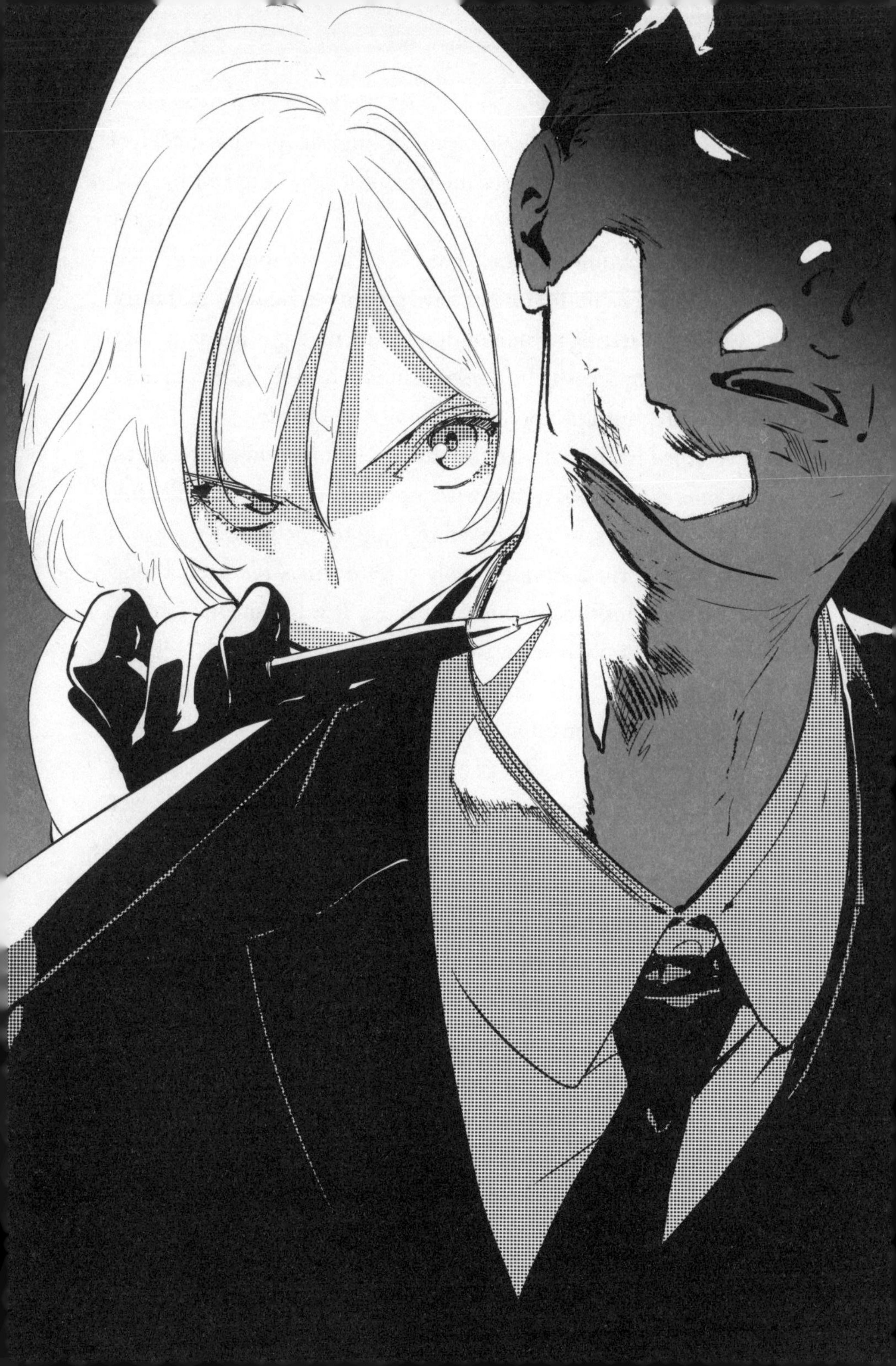

"Did you need me?" I said, again in English.

"It seems you're not rusty," he replied.

"Show me your ID card."

"It's me. Have you forgotten me?"

"You could be in disguise or have gotten plastic surgery. Hurry up," I said, not letting my guard down. The man put his hand into his pocket. From the way he'd been walking, he didn't seem to have a gun in there, but I gripped the ballpoint pen harder.

I watched his movements carefully. The man took out a black leather pass case. It had a card with a portrait on it to help identify its bearer. When I saw it, I relaxed my grip on the pen.

The man turned around slowly towards me. "It's been a long time," he said, this time in fluent Japanese. It was someone I knew. I'd worked for him when I was in America.

The ID said "FBI" in large letters. The official name was Federal Bureau of Investigation. It was, of course, an American police organization. It was also my old workplace. I'd changed my citizenship to American in order to work there, so right now I technically wasn't Japanese, but American.

"Oliver, fancy running into you in Japan."

"It's no coincidence. I came to Japan specifically to see you."

"Is there some rule that says if you want to see someone who quit, you have to tail them?"

Oliver Roseland. Thirty-seven years old. My former boss. To be honest, he wasn't a man I wanted to see outside of work. Other people's opinions might differ, though.

"That outfit looks good on you. It's what they call 'Japanese Kawaii,' right? Have you managed to fit in at a Japanese school?"

"You don't have to ask questions when you're not interested in the answers."

"It's a shame you left the bureau. You were good at your job."

"Thanks." I didn't believe him. I knew him too well for that.

"How's your mother's illness?"

"Her Alzheimer's is getting worse," I said, as expressionlessly as I could. "She doesn't even remember that she has a daughter at all, let alone who I am."

"I see. Does your psychometry still work?"

"Well enough." I felt like I was undergoing an interview. It didn't feel like he was here to catch up on old times.

Psychometry. That power was what had gotten me a job at the FBI at my age, and it was what had let me keep it.

In my case, I would go into a mental space that looked like a movie theater and watch the memories of an object appear on a screen. I was often told it was an overly elaborate way of doing things, and I agreed. But it was something I needed to do if I wanted to separate my memories from those of other people. "Fusion" always followed "synchronization."

When you read somebody's memories, you would become them, and then not only would your memories mix, but so would your personality. It was a common problem for people with this power, I'd heard.

When I was little, I'd often get very confused after using my powers. That's why I created that mental movie theater—as a way to protect my mind.

"What do you want? You haven't come here just to see how I'm doing."

"I want you to use your power to help me."

"You came all the way from America to Japan to call me back?"

"That's right."

"Did you forget why I quit?"

"I'm not going to tell you to come back to America."

"What?"

"I want you to take over the work of an agent who was working in Japan."

I wasn't expecting that, so I let my confusion show on my face. "An agent, working in Japan?"

"Agent Moritsuka."

Moritsuka?!

Shun Moritsuka. A man who always looked like an idiot but was as clever as they came. His powers of observation and intuition exceeded those of anyone else I knew.

I'd known Moritsuka since he'd come to Japan to work on a certain case. Since we were both Japanese, he'd often come to chat with me for five or ten minutes about nothing in particular and then leave. He was a weird guy. Moritsuka wasn't with the FBI very long, but from the way everyone around him acted, I could tell he excelled at his job.

"He came back to the FBI?"

"No. But he was working with us on this case."

Why would they need me to take over a case Moritsuka was on?

"They got Moritsuka."

What?! What did he just say? Moritsuka? They got him? They got him? Did that mean…

He was dead?

"You heard about the 256 bodies they found in Inokashira Park, right? One of them was Moritsuka's."

"What?!"

How? Suicide? An accident? Or murder?

If it was murder, then who...?

Calm down. Remember the training you got when you joined the FBI. I tensed my limbs and focused my mind to calm my anxiety. I closed my eyes and took a quick breath.

I didn't know for sure that Moritsuka was dead yet. It was possible that Oliver was bluffing, or that his information was bad. I needed to stay calm.

"Are you sure about this?"

"The information came from the Musashino police, the place where Moritsuka was working. His co-workers ID'd the body. They're sure."

"What was he working on?"

"He was looking into an NGO that belonged to a certain organization, but it's not clear if they were behind it. All we know is that he's gone."

From the way he was talking, "murder" was the safe assumption. I repeated the meaning of this in my mind and bit my lip. "So you're saying that all 256 were murders, not suicides?"

"Moritsuka had no reason to kill himself. Thus, we think it was murder. There's no other evidence besides that."

In other words, they barely knew anything.

"HQ is in an uproar. Agent Moritsuka was extremely useful in any case that involved the supernatural. Losing him is going to hurt."

"Moritsuka..." I'd had no idea he'd died in the Inokashira

incident. I hadn't realized it, but Moritsuka was in Kichijoji, too. Maybe I'd passed him on the street. "And you want me to take over his work?"

"You want revenge for him too, right?"

Revenge, huh? I stared down at my glove-covered hands.

Oliver was right. I owed my life to Moritsuka. Right now, I just barely had control over my psychometry. But before I'd met Moritsuka at the FBI, my power had been more or less running wild. Since I couldn't control it, the memories of anything I touched would come flooding into me. I couldn't even live my daily life, and all my efforts had been devoted to not touching anything.

"You can't control your power, can you?" he'd asked. "If you don't figure out a way, eventually it'll kill you."

After I'd already talked with Moritsuka several times, I'd had a heart attack one day. It had never happened when I was little, but a while after I joined the FBI, I learned that my heart was in awful shape. The FBI's doctors took a look at me, but all they could tell me was that they didn't know why it was happening. For some reason, Moritsuka was able to tell instantly that my heart attack was due to overusing my psychometry.

"Your psychometry puts a pretty big strain on your body, I think," he'd told me. "The FBI doesn't want you quitting, so they're hiding that from you. That's just how all big organizations are, you know. Terrible, just terrible."

When he told me this, I'd felt betrayed by the FBI. I was so shocked that I hadn't slept a wink that night. I could tell that my whole body was screaming, but since the bureau needed my power, I couldn't stop using it.

The next day, Moritsuka came to me and said, "Here, I brought you a present." He put a pair of black gloves on me. "These are magic cat's-paw gloves that can temporarily seal away your psychometry."

I had no idea what he was talking about. Sure, they definitely weren't normal gloves. The palm and fingers were covered with shock absorber pads that looked like a cat's paw. Still, I knew that it would take more than some fabric and fake paws to seal away my power. I knew that better than anyone. I'd had this power since I was a kid. I'd tried all kinds of things to seal it away. Wearing gloves to stop it was the first thing I'd tried, and of course it hadn't worked at all.

When I told him that, Moritsuka just laughed. "Did you know that sometimes, people can get better just because they believe something? The trick is to believe that those gloves can temporarily seal away your power."

That was impossible, but when I told him that...

"But you were already able to protect your mind by making a movie theater, weren't you? So why can't you believe that these gloves are magic?"

His words were enough to make me understand. After that, I was able to learn to temporarily seal my power with the gloves. As long as I wore them, my powers wouldn't activate when I touched something. Because of that, the stress on my body was reduced. It was thanks to Moritsuka that I was still alive.

The cat's-paw gloves Moritsuka had given me were still at my house. They were my treasure. So when I heard he was dead, it was natural for me to want revenge. But what did the FBI want with me? I'd been out of there for a while. Why would they want me to take over for Moritsuka?

"Do you think I'm capable of this?"

"You're the only one who is."

In other words, they were counting on my psychometry. I thought it over silently. If I went back to being an agent, I'd have to use my power a lot. If I did that, my heart would…

"We're willing to pay for all your mother's medical expenses. We'll also provide somebody to take care of her needs."

Why was he bringing that up now?

"That sounds like a threat to me." If I quit, or started to slack off, one of my mother's caregivers could turn from a nurse into an assassin.

Oliver ignored me. "We're also willing to make accommodations for your health."

That was the reason I'd quit the FBI. My body hadn't recovered or improved. No, it was slowly getting worse.

Hypertrophic cardiomyopathy: a disease where the muscles of the heart enlarge to the point where they can't send blood to the rest of the body. The positioning of the enlargement in my heart meant that the Batista procedure wasn't an option. The only thing that could save me right now was a heart transplant. It was a difficult procedure, but without it, my heart's muscles would eventually lose the ability to contract. I had two years left, at best. If I was lucky, I might live to see twenty, but no better than that.

I wanted to spend the rest of my short life in peace. That's why I'd come back to Japan.

"I…" I grit my teeth and gently put my hand against my chest, which constantly hurt with a dull ache.

Oliver's "accommodations" were probably a reference to a heart transplant in America. If that was possible, it would add years to my life.

"I don't think it's a bad deal," he said.

I knew Oliver didn't like me. He kept his distance in the same way the girls at Seimei High avoided me. I understood why he wouldn't like me; I could find in thirty minutes what would take him a week of difficult investigations. Yet he'd come all the way to Japan personally to ask for me to join the bureau again.

The FBI must have really had its back against the wall. What had Moritsuka been looking into?

"...Moritsuka."

He was dead. He was gone. Whenever I'd run into him at the FBI's offices, he would always smile that innocent smile of his and offer me a piece of the candy he kept in his pocket. He was almost like Santa Claus.

But now he was gone.

I took another deep breath and stared hard into Oliver's eyes. "I'll do it. Tell me about the case Moritsuka was working on."

I wasn't doing this for the FBI. I was going back to being an FBI agent for Moritsuka's sake.

PARANORMAL SCIENCE NVL.

Occultic;Nine

オカルティック・ナイン

THERE IS NO SUCH THING AS THE "OCCULT." IT CAN ALL BE DISPROVED BY SCIENCE.
ONLY THOSE WHO HAVE ACCEPTED EVERYTHING
HAVE THE RIGHT TO KNOW THE TRUTH.

I clutched my familiar "Peter"—the one that had patchwork-colored teeth and looked like a mouse—and sank into the sofa in my living room. I was so tired. The last few days had been mentally exhausting. When I got up in the morning, I was so exhausted I couldn't stand up. Even running a comb through my hair felt like it required too much effort.

I stretched out an unsteady hand for the remote and turned on the TV. It was a big TV, appropriate for the luxurious living room, but compared to the latest high-definition models it was bulky and ugly. The family had been using it for twenty years. We'd had to hook an HD tuner to it to keep it alive at all. It was like a zombie.

It had originally been brought from somewhere by my brother. Since we hadn't had a TV until he'd brought it, I'd spent my younger years without one. I remembered being so excited when he set it up.

I loved everything that my brother did. To me, he was like a god. Or maybe even more than that.

He was my world. But…

"That detective…" I saw his face in my mind and found myself whispering hatefully.

He had come to my shop several days ago. He was a very rude man. It was thanks to him I'd been so tired these past few days. When I thought back to how disgusting I'd looked and how much I'd embarrassed myself just because he'd brought up my brother, it made me feel terribly depressed.

The world displayed on the TV was so colorful and alive compared to the faded gloom of the house. I stared at it and thought back to when the detective had visited several days ago.

"My name is Moritsuka, and I'm with the Musashino police. That's Moritsuka, okay? Not 'zu.' Nice to meet you." The tiny man in the trench coat had come into my shop right after I'd opened. "I knew your brother back when he was alive."

I was so shocked when I heard him say those words that I'd told him all about my memories of my brother.

Well… not all of them.

"I see. So your brother's room is the same as it was."

"Yes," I replied hesitantly.

As I was talking to him, I realized there was no way my brother would ever spend time with a shallow, callous man like this. This Moritsuka guy was lying. His goal must have been to bring up my brother and cause me distress.

"Hmm, but doesn't it get all dusty? Do you clean it? Knowing you, I suppose you would. This shop is very clean, after all. Man, I love the atmosphere in here!" He grinned and looked around as if he wanted me to watch him do it.

The House of Crimson had no open windows. The only light source was a single exposed bulb. There was no way to tell in the gloom whether the place was properly being cleaned or not.

I stared at Moritsuka's face. He looked a lot younger than I usually envisioned a detective. If someone were to tell me he was younger than I was, I'd probably believe them.

He doesn't look like a customer, I'd thought. *A short man in a beige trench coat. He looks like a kid, but he sure doesn't move like one.*

That's how the devil had once described the person who was sneaking around my store. The description matched. It was the same person... probably.

"So what do you want?"

Moritsuka's attitude was upsetting me. He seemed to be doing it deliberately, and I was angry at him for bringing up my brother. I wanted him to tell me what he was here for and then leave.

"Oh, how rude of me. Actually, I have a question for you."

"If it's about my brother, I've already—"

"The Kotoribako. You know what that is, right?" Moritsuka interrupted me. He ignored my obvious surprise and continued. "It was found on the grounds of Enmeiji yesterday. An obviously handmade—and very poorly so—wooden box. You can imagine what I'm talking about, right?"

"No," I lied. Due to the nature of my job, I knew a lot about old rituals like that. I'd once researched the legend of the Kotoribako.

"Oh, really? The investigators say it was a wooden box, just big enough for one person to hold."

I didn't respond.

"The box itself was poorly made, but when I looked at it

carefully, I saw that it was like some kind of puzzle. So I Googled it and found that it looked just like a box called a 'Kotoribako.'"

That I knew well. The devil had told me about a white boy at Enmeiji, holding the Kotoribako—or more precisely, something that looked like the Kotoribako. That was what Moritsuka was trying to get me to talk about. But how did he know I was involved, in a small way, with the Enmeiji incident?

"Then you have no idea? Where would someone even make such a thing?"

"I couldn't say. I have no idea."

"I'm sure." Moritsuka gave up easily. It was as if he wanted to say he knew that's how I would answer. "They're supposedly made in Hakone, as a kind of local arts-and-crafts thing. But the ones they make there are a different size, and a different, well…everything."

The Kotoribako.

This detective knew exactly what it was, and he was asking me about it anyway. Everything he did seemed to be designed to test me. As the subject of his "tests," I was starting to get angry. Moritsuka knew I was getting mad too, and he was counting on it. I felt a slight urge to vomit.

"By the way, did you make all those dolls there yourself? They're very well-made." Moritsuka pointed at my familiars, which were lined up on the shelf behind me.

"Thank you."

"I'm a bit embarrassed to say it, but I'm not good with my hands. I've always wanted to make a figure based on a *Vanguard* card, but I doubt I'll ever be able to do it. Oh, but it's always important to try, isn't it? Where do you buy the materials for those things? Yuzawaya?"

The detective walked around the table and went to touch one of them.

"Would you please not touch them? Those are my familiars. I use them in my black magic rituals."

"Oh, how rude of me. I'm sorry, I'm just the kind of guy who needs to pick something up and feel it in his hands." The detective bowed and walked back. "It's the same with clothes and shoes, you know? Lately, there are more places to buy them online, and a lot of people just buy based off pictures, but I can't believe that anybody would do that. If you don't try it on yourself, you don't know if it's really for you."

He kept talking and talking. I took a brief glance around the shop, half-ignoring him.

I couldn't hear the devil's voice. I couldn't sense him, either. Was he here, but simply silently observing me? Or had he not come at all today?

"Detective, if there's nothing else I can do for you, I'll have to ask you to leave."

"Oh, wait, wait," the detective said. "Um, well, inside that box they found at Enmeiji was a corpse that was all smashed up like mincemeat." Evidently, he had no intention of sugarcoating his words.

I may have been running a black magic agency, but I was still a teenage girl. Then again, refusing to show the slightest degree of consideration was probably part of his plan as well.

"We were able to ID the body based on her possessions. It was Chizu Kawabata, a local high school girl. We're waiting for forensics to come back with more details. Does anything strike you as curious about this?"

"Yes. I'm curious why you're asking me."

There was no reason for this detective to be watching me. Of course, I knew about what had happened at Enmeiji, but I hadn't learned about it in real time. And I definitely hadn't gone to Enmeiji myself.

Was it really right to say that I was involved? Or was this Moritsuka uninterested in the Enmeiji murder and simply planning to arrest me for the crime of using a devil to curse people?

"I'd hoped that since you know a lot about black magic and curses, you might have noticed something that we missed."

"Black magic is my specialty, yes, but why me? There are many people who are more famous, aren't there?"

"Yes, but actually, when I looked at the phone book in the station, your shop's name was at the top of the list."

"My shop isn't listed in the phone book."

"Oh, it's not?"

Moritsuka had told an obvious lie and didn't seem in the least perturbed to be called out on it. His attitude was bad enough, but more than anything, his smile was upsetting me. He covered all his emotions with that smile and forced his enemy to let their guard down. It was like a light in the darkness luring moths to their death.

What a terrible heart this man had. It was the exact opposite of my brother's gentle, encompassing smile.

"By the way, how have things been lately?"

"Things?" I asked.

"Cursed anyone?"

"That's my job."

"Have any of your clients recently been especially vengeful? Any politicians plunking down huge sums of cash? Or perhaps…"

He stopped himself and looked at me. The smile was still on his lips.

"Or perhaps someone came to you with a giant pile of hair and asked you to kill its owner?"

The sharp light in his eyes broke through my expressionless shell, and I grimaced. He knew about that job. He must've spent a lot of time hanging around here.

"I'm afraid I can't share any information about my clients."

"Aww, come on. Tell me. I'll keep it off the record."

"I refuse. Is that all?"

"Hmm… I suppose there's one more thing, while I'm here. Ria Minase."

"Yes."

He caught me off guard. He'd used my real name, and I'd answered. I groaned to myself. He'd used my real name deliberately. But why? Did he just want me to know he'd done his research on me? If so, what was the point of telling me that?

"Have you ever heard of 'Kodoku'?"

"No."

"Put simply, it's a type of spell where you seal a pot filled with all kinds of insects and make them kill each other until only the strongest remains," he explained.

"I've never heard of it. My agency only deals in Western magics."

"So you know that the Kodoku is Eastern magic. Aww, and you just told me you didn't know, too."

He'd caught me off guard again.

An emotional girl was a poor match for my logical and gentle older brother. I resolved to do better as I lowered my eyes.

"I pride myself on being well-informed on Western magic, so I assumed that if I didn't know it, it must be something else."

"I see. And so you thought it must be Eastern magic."

"No. I thought it might be from the mainland as well."

"Ahh, yeah. That's possible too, isn't it? You've sure got me there." He was clearly doing this on purpose.

"You certainly know a lot about magic."

"Nah, in the world of 2D culture, it's well-known."

I still had no idea what he was actually here for.

It felt I was being slowly strangled by an invisible thread. There was no need for me to feel pain. There was no reason for me to feel guilty.

So why did it feel like I was being slowly pushed into a corner?

It was like a curse.

Stay calm. Stay calm. If I let him scare me, I was just doing what he wanted. I needed to deal with this properly, like a black magic agent.

"So what does this Kodoku have to do with the box that was found at the temple? Don't tell me that the person who was found dead inside was a victim of it."

"No, it doesn't feel like they killed people to try to make a Kodoku. The body showed no signs of life. It seemed to have been torn apart after death. But there's one thing I'm curious about. Supposedly, if you use the last surviving insect of a Kodoku as the vessel for your spell, it vastly enhances the spell's power. By sacrificing the disgusting creature that fought all the other insects in the pot, ate their corpses, and slurped up their urine and feces, you can make your magic more than twice as strong."

"That's very interesting," I said, not interested at all.

"Whoa. You don't sound interested at all." Moritsuka shrugged. Did he look surprised because he expected me to act more interested? What a ridiculous joke.

"My black magic does not use corpses."

"That's right. You use hair, don't you? It didn't say that on your web page, though."

"If you ever make an official request for a job, I'll tell you then."

"Hmm... unfortunately, there's no one I want to kill right now."

"Then please leave." I was finally able to say it.

Any more would simply be a waste of time and a source of stress. No matter what he said now, I wanted him to know that I had no intention of listening.

"Oh. Can I ask one last question, then?"

"No. Please leave."

Moritsuka ignored me. Beneath the light of the exposed bulb, the young detective's cap cast a shadow on his face, making his expression hard to read.

"Do you think it's a crime to kill someone with black magic?"

Who was he talking about? Did he think I'd been responsible for the Enmeiji murder?

He was so wrong that I almost laughed. "All I do is pray. I don't do the deed myself. The deed is done by the hand of the devil, who is the lord of evil."

"Hmm, so I could probably string you and this imaginary devil up as co-conspirators."

Imaginary…devil?

"If you'd like to try, go ahead."

It would only end with him being laughed at.

"By the way," he said. I realized that the deliberately cheerful tone was gone from Moritsuka's voice. "How did you know Chizu Kawamoto was at Enmeiji?"

"The devil told me. He said there was strong karma gathered there."

"Where did you meet this imaginary devil? Is he someone you can trust?"

"I believe I asked you to leave."

"Now, now. This is really my last question," he said. He pushed up the brim of his cap and leaned forward, close enough that I could feel his breath.

Then…he whispered in my ear.

"You don't really believe in devils, do you?"

I was struck dumb.

In the tiny, gloomy room, with no light at all from the outside, Moritsuka laughed as if he could read my mind. But the eyes that were staring at me weren't smiling at all.

"Ria Minase. You loved your brother, didn't you? It's nice to have a sibling. I always wanted a cute little sister who would look up to me."

"What are you trying to say?"

Slowly, a cold sensation began to creep upwards from my toes. I shivered and looked away from him.

Don't touch me! I wanted to scream.

In fact, his hands were still in his coat pockets, and there was no way he could touch me.

I was trapped in the spider web of his words, and suddenly I found myself unable to move a muscle. That's how it felt.

"Your relationship, Minase, with this imaginary devil, seems like the exact opposite of the ones I'm familiar with from black magic. Like you're the servant, and the devil is the master?"

I simply stared at him.

"So here's what I'm trying to say: Isn't this what you were always looking for? A master who could take the place of your brother? And that's how you're keeping yourself stable. Or rather, content."

Like a snake, the coldness that had been rising up from my toes coiled itself around my neck. I almost screamed.

"What you wanted wasn't knowledge of black magic, or loyal familiars who would carry out your will. It was someone who would make you certain that you were really there, that you existed, when sometimes it didn't feel like you did. Am I wrong?"

I found myself unable to react.

"You wanted something like your brother, someone who would accept you unconditionally when you were depressed. Wouldn't you have been happy with anything that fit those conditions? A man, or even a devil—"

"*Leave!*" I pushed Moritsuka as hard as I could.

"Whoa! You scared me!" Moritsuka fell backwards and landed on the ground.

I started throwing things, antique candlestick holders and pen stands, at him, but they didn't hit him. Instead, they crashed against the walls and floor.

"What are you doing?! You're interfering with the duties of a public servant!"

"Leave! Leave!" I was so angry I was panting. How long had it been since I'd raised my voice like this? The only thing I wanted to do was curse the detective in front of me until he was dead. "Get out of here! Now!"

Moritsuka shrugged a little and stood up. He brushed the dust off his coat.

"I'm sorry. Looks like I pushed a little too hard. I won't prosecute you for attacking me, so please forgive me for being rude. Goodbye," he said, and then he waved as he left the shop. As I listened to the sound of his shoes going down the stairs, I grabbed Peter, the familiar nearest to me.

The devil didn't appear in my shop that day. Neither did a single customer. So I didn't know how long I spent there, shivering.

It wasn't something I wanted to remember. I bit my lip and shook the memories from my mind.

At some point, a huge list of names had begun to appear on the TV screen. It was a list of the 256 victims of the Inokashira incident.

How much meaning was there in each of those names? What difference was there between these names and the ones written by my clients?

As I thought about it...

Suddenly, amidst the list of names...

I saw it.

"Ria Minase."

"Oh..." Even though I called myself Aria Kurenaino now, my

real name wasn't something I could easily forget, and I recognized it instantly on the screen.

It was the name I'd thrown away. The name of my brother's little sister. It was a name I wasn't worthy of, now that I'd made a pact with a devil.

I chuckled a little and looked up at the ceiling of my living room, where a useless, elaborate chandelier hung.

"I'd thought maybe that was the case."

I didn't feel like trying to convince myself that it wasn't true. Really, it felt like it made sense. The despair was actually kind of refreshing.

"I can't believe my wish came true like this…"

I'd wanted to die. If I died, I thought I could see my brother again. I'd waited so long for the day to come.

But now that I was actually dead, I still hadn't seen my brother. The person I'd most wanted to see in the afterlife was nowhere to be found.

"Oh, how maddeningly enticing, and how maddeningly cruel…" I covered my face with both hands. This must be hell, not heaven. It was the perfect place for a girl who'd clung to a devil for help.

What was my brother thinking when he looked down on me from heaven? It felt like I was even further from my brother than when I'd been clinging to life.

"You have no right to that yet."

I remembered what the devil had told me about dying when we'd first met.

Paranormal Science NVL

Occultic;Nine

オカルティック・ナイン

There is no such thing as the "Occult." It can all be disproved by science.
Only those who have accepted everything
have the right to know the truth.

My dorm was a ten-minute walk from Inokashira Park Station, the one next to Kichijoji Station.

It was two stories high and a little old, but it had a cafeteria that offered breakfast and dinner. Most of the residents were college kids who had come from the countryside to Tokyo, but I'd lived overseas, so I was given special permission to stay here. Since I was going to Seimei University, I wouldn't be moving out this year, either.

After I got back from school, I opened the closet and tried to find something to wear. Oliver wanted me to start working with the FBI again immediately. When I'd agreed, he'd acted fast.

"A detective from the Musashino Police will be at your dorm in an hour. Meet him there."

That was all he'd said before he left.

"He doesn't care about my schedule at all, huh?" I whispered. But I'd known what Oliver was like when I started working with him, and I wasn't really surprised.

I took off my school uniform and quickly changed into my civilian clothes. I needed to wear something that wouldn't attract attention at a crime scene. I had a child's face and a small body, so I wanted something that wouldn't make me look like a child. Unfortunately, nothing I had with me qualified.

When I was with the FBI, I could wear a jacket with the bureau's name printed in big letters on the back. Did the Japanese police have anything like that? If they did, they probably wouldn't give it to me.

I finished changing and checked myself in the mirror. I'd chosen a white and blue jacket to wear over a one-piece dress, and I looked to make sure there was no obvious dirt on my black leggings. It would have been better if I had a suit, but since I was now a Japanese high school girl, I didn't need one, and it wouldn't look good on me anyway. I was going to have to go buy one now, though.

Compared to FBI agents, how would Japanese detectives treat me?

"Back then, I really was a kid…"

I wanted to believe that as I'd gotten older, I'd started to look more like a grown-up, but the truth was that I hadn't gotten much taller at all. Maybe it was because I didn't eat much, or maybe it was because of my condition, but I hadn't really grown at all.

No matter what I looked like in the eyes of the Japanese detectives, it didn't matter right now anyway. My one priority was to take over Moritsuka's case and solve it.

The last thing I did was put on my black cat's-paw gloves. They weren't the white ones I usually used, but the ones Moritsuka had given me.

The feeling of the paw pads on the palms brought back memories. I hadn't worn these since I worked for the FBI. When I put them on, I felt just a little bit better.

After fifteen minutes of waiting in front of the dorm, a black car appeared. A heavily-built man in a suit got out from the driver's side.

His suit was beaten up, and his hair was kind of a mess. He had an unshaven beard on his chin and a cigarette in his mouth. If this were a movie, he'd be less an FBI agent and more like a crusty old local police detective. Just from looking at him, he seemed pretty stubborn and hard-headed.

Our eyes met.

"Oh, you're Kizaki?"

"Yes. Are you from the Musashino police?"

The man nodded. He looked annoyed. "I'm Shinoyama, from the Musashino police."

"Nice to meet you." I bowed, but Detective Shinoyama just looked at me suspiciously. But I was used to that.

"I'm FBI Agent Asuna Kizaki."

To drive the point home, I handed him the temporary ID card Oliver had given me earlier. It had the stamp of the FBI Director on it. Oliver said he'd prepared it in advance. The photo was one from when I'd been in America.

Shinoyama only glanced at the ID. He'd probably already been briefed. "Get in."

He extinguished the cigarette in a portable ashtray, then got back into the car and turned it on. I decided to ride in the back instead of the front.

It stank. The whole car stank of cigarette smoke. I had to deal with it all the way to the station.

The media was gathered in front of Musashino Police Station. Some of the reporters were broadcasting live already. After all the big crimes going on in Kichijoji, everybody was on edge. The same was true of Mitaka, where Musashino Police Station was located.

Speaking from experience, I expected the same atmosphere inside the station itself, but once I stepped past the front door, I was surprised by how empty it felt.

"There don't seem to be many people here. Is it usually like this?" I asked, before I even realized I'd done so. It was my first time in a Japanese police station, so I couldn't be sure.

"Everybody's out now dealing with the Inokashira incident, and the others, too. It's rare to have this many major crimes at once," Shinoyama said without looking back at me.

We got into the elevator and he pushed the button for the fourth floor.

"By 'others,' do you mean the murder of the professor at Seimei?"

"That's part of it. The other would be the dismembered body of a girl that was found at Enmeiji. That was a murder, too."

I felt like I'd heard that story on the news, but I didn't know the details. "Any connection to the mass suicides?"

"None that we've found yet."

"Tell me the details." I stared straight into his eyes as I spoke. He sighed in resignation and told me.

According to him, a wooden box, forty centimeters per side, had been found on the grounds of Enmeiji Temple. It was filled with tiny pieces of what used to be a person. They hadn't ID'd the body yet, but from the objects that were left in the box, they believed it likely that it was a girl from Seimei High.

That was my school. I'd had no idea that over the past few weeks, multiple people from Seimei Academy had died.

There was also a rumor that several of the suicides were Seimei people. Even if it was too soon to assume they were connected, I couldn't help but feel that something terrifying was happening in this town.

Shinoyama led me to a room marked "Meeting Room #2." It was a decent-sized room with several tables and chairs lined up. He told me to wait there a while and then came back with another detective—this one's name was Kozaki—carrying three cardboard boxes.

"These are Moritsuka's things."

The three boxes were placed on one of the tables.

"Let me take a look."

The first contained a wallet and cellphone, kept in plastic bags to preserve them as evidence. His favorite cap was in there, too. I'd seen him wearing it at the FBI. He'd told me he wore it out of respect for an anime character named Zenigata. I'd even seen him wearing it in summer, so it must have been really important to him.

The second box held a small amount of clothes and paperwork. The third box, the heaviest, held...

"Anime DVDs, manga, and... What's this?"

"Cards. Supposedly it's something called a 'trading card game,'" Kozaki answered. He was a little younger and thinner than Shinoyama, and he looked kind of nervous.

Moritsuka had more cards than anything else in his things. There were hundreds of cards, carefully placed in six binders.

"All this was found in Moritsuka's desk?"

Shinoyama pointed at the box holding the wallet and phone. "That box was taken from his house, but the others, yes."

That would mean he kept the DVDs and cards at his desk at the police station. He was a government worker, but he brought his personal possessions to work and played with them? Sure, Moritsuka was always a bit odd, and he always kept pieces of candy in his coat pocket, but that wasn't quite like the Moritsuka I knew. He'd been working here at the station in Mitaka for almost a year, though.

I'd been going to the high school one station over. If only I'd known he was so close... I would have come to see him.

I bit my lip and tried to pick what objects to use my power on. I could use my psychometry on anything, be it human or object. Naturally, there was a difference between the two in how many memories I could read. If I had a metal object that the person kept with him at all times, I could replay memories very clearly, but nothing I found fit that criteria. The fastest way was probably the phone, then.

The battery must have run out, because when I pressed the power button, nothing happened. However, psychometry didn't need electricity.

Shinoyama and Kozaki stared at me silently.

"I'm going to concentrate for a minute. Don't talk to me, please," I said, then I took off my gloves and closed my eyes.

Begin the performance.

I imagined an empty movie theater. The projector started to roll.

Moritsuka's face appeared up close on the screen. There was no warning, so I almost screamed.

He was staring into his phone's camera. It felt like it had been a long, long time since I'd seen his face. He looked young enough that if someone told me he was my age, I'd probably believe them, and his face hadn't changed a bit since he was in the FBI.

I stopped myself from crying, somehow, and ran the film back into the past.

"Huh? The battery's run out." Moritsuka had just stuck the phone onto its charging cradle, but he must have put it on wrong, because it didn't start charging. He kept chuckling and adjusting it. Then he headed towards the bathroom.

I stopped the performance and opened my eyes. This phone hadn't recorded the moment of his death.

"Moritsuka left his wallet and his phone at home, and then went to Inokashira Park to kill himself?"

If the phone had been found at his home, not near his body, that would explain things. If he'd gone to kill himself, that wouldn't have been that surprising, but...

Oliver had said he'd been killed. Did that mean that he'd been kidnapped from his home?

"Listen... Kizaki, was that your name?" Kozaki asked me, sounding surprised. "What were you just doing?"

"Psychometry. Agent Oliver didn't tell you?"

"No." Shinoyama shook his head as well.

"It's the power to read the memories of a person or thing by touching them."

"Didn't they used to do that on TV?"

Shinoyama's eyes went wider. "The FBI is really doing that stuff, huh? I thought it was just something they made up." He believed me more easily than I thought he would.

"You believe me?"

"To be honest, not in the slightest. But if the FBI sent you, you must be good for something. If nothing else, Moritsuka wasn't holding his phone or his wallet when he died. That much you got right."

So my guess was correct, then.

"Thank you."

"Right now, we need all the help we can get. That's all."

That meant the investigation into all these cases wasn't going well.

"Where are the things he was carrying with him when he died?'

"In the temporary morgue. Not everybody's been identified yet, so we can't get permission to take them out."

The temporary morgue. That would have to be my next stop, then.

"Do the Japanese police intend to call this a suicide?"

"That's what the brass thinks, it seems."

"That Moritsuka's death was a suicide?"

Shinoyama sighed a little and scratched his head. "To be honest, we didn't really understand Moritsuka. He died without us learning anything about him."

Kozaki's reaction was similar. Both of them seemed to be telling the truth. Moritsuka was the type who preferred to act on his own. Maybe he didn't have any deep connections with the

Musashino police.

I moved Moritsuka's phone back into the cardboard box. Then I decided to look for other things that I could use for my psychometry. I rummaged through the box with the DVDs and manga and found one thing that interested me.

"A book?"

It was the size of a magazine, but much thinner than the other manga. It didn't seem to have many pages at all. The drawings seemed kind of amateurish, too.

The Bottom of the Deep Water. That was the title. There were two men on the cover. I flipped through it, more out of curiosity than anything.

I gasped a little in surprise. On the pages inside, the male characters were naked and embracing each other.

"Why?"

"Did Moritsuka swing that way, maybe?"

Shinoyama and Kozaki both seemed a little confused, too.

Was this what Moritsuka liked? I'd never heard anything about that. If he had been, I wouldn't have told him it was wrong, but…

The question was, why did he have this thing?

I looked through the rest of his things, but the only book of that kind was this one. Out of all the manga and anime he had, it stood out from the rest.

I remembered how Moritsuka had behaved when he was at the FBI. Often he would do things that looked like playing around to everyone else. But every time he did something like that, he would always solve the case immediately afterward.

"This is Moritsuka magic, you see."

He'd say it like he was joking, but maybe there was some kind of meaning to it.

"Did Moritsuka tell you anything about this book?"

"Come to think of it…"

"He did, then?"

"When Isayuki Hashigami was killed, Moritsuka was the first on the scene. I remember him saying something really strange. Something about how the way the professor was killed matched up with what was in some doujin manga. Maybe that's the manga?"

"A doujin manga?" I went back to the start and began to read through it again. "What did Moritsuka say matched between the case and this manga?"

"Hmm… what was it again?"

"The tooth," Kozaki answered. "He said the tooth being removed was the same."

"The tooth… here it is." I found the page halfway through the book. There were several panels devoted to a scene of a man raping the corpse of a man he'd killed and then ripping out an implanted tooth with a knife. "Dr. Hashigami had an implant that was removed?"

"Yeah. Forensics said that there were no signs that he was alive when it was done. Which means—"

"Which means it was removed after death, right?"

The media had said nothing about the tooth. The police must have been keeping it to themselves.

"What have you been doing to follow up on this?"

"We haven't followed up."

"Why?"

Shinoyama looked away awkwardly. "When Moritsuka gave us the report, we laughed it off as a joke and ignored it."

"I see."

The rest of the force had ignored him, so Moritsuka had decided to investigate it himself, perhaps? If that was the case, then did the killer find him and kill him too, before he could tell anyone else?

I flipped through the pages some more. As I did, a single card fell out and landed on the floor. I picked it up and saw that its design was the same as the trading cards in the binders. The picture was of a European-style dragon, and the card itself shimmered rainbow colors in the fluorescent lights.

Why was this card stuck in the manga, instead of filed away?

I suddenly felt anxious. I put the manga down on the desk and clutched the card with both hands as if praying.

Begin the performance.

On the screen, Moritsuka was staring at the card… no, at me. In the theater.

"Umm… ahem. This card, which was placed inside the doujin manga, will be a critical piece of evidence in the search for the killer of Dr. Hashigami, professor from Seimei University."

The way he was talking was very strange. It was as if he was talking to the card itself.

"This manga depicts accurately what happened after the professor's murder. Oh, by the way, it came out at last year's Comiket. It wasn't drawn after the murder. It was drawn before."

What…was this? Why was Moritsuka saying all this to himself? There was nobody else in the room he was in. He wasn't talking to anyone on his phone. Who was he talking to?

And then I realized…

Was this…?

"This is just my intuition talking, but I think this book holds a lot of secrets. You could say it's like…" Moritsuka sighed a little.

And then he said…

"Like a book of prophecy."

His expression was serious. There was no trace of his usual childish, easygoing manner.

"I think I'll be okay again, but I'm going to leave clues just in case something happens. Not…that I really want to think about what that something might be."

I was right. The memories of this card…

Moritsuka wasn't talking to himself.

He was talking to a psychometer, like me?

On the screen, he smiled.

Even at the worst crime scenes, Moritsuka's laughs were always filled with cheer. This was just like the time I'd been brought to a certain crime scene and been terrified of the stench of blood and screams of the other agents. It was Moritsuka's smile that had cheered me up.

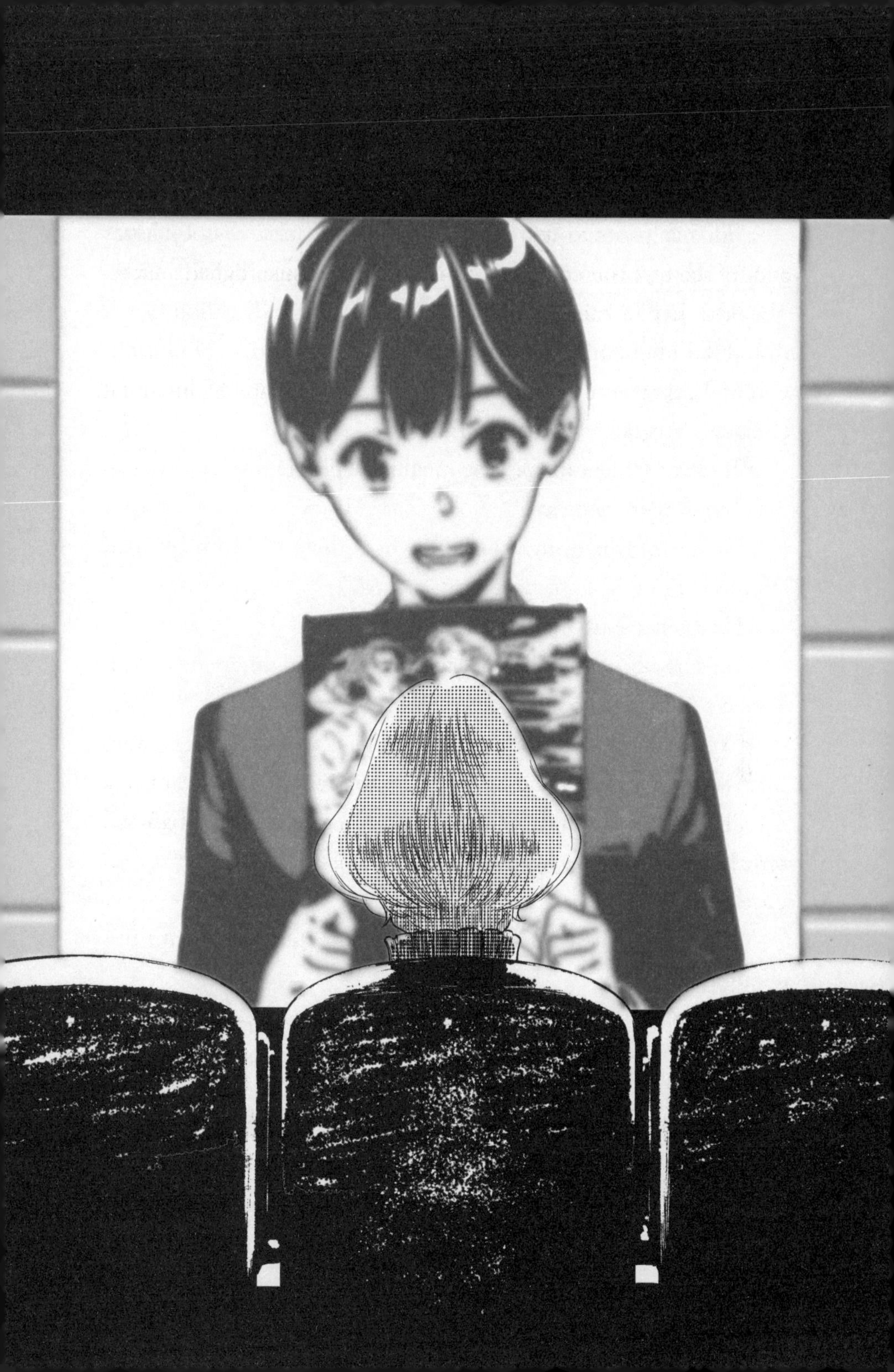

I'd never see that smile again.

But he'd handed the baton to me like this.

"I'll tell you the two things I'm investigating that I'm sure about. The first is Ririka Nishizono and this manga that she wrote. The other is FM-KCZ, a mini-FM radio station in Kichijoji. Well, that one I'm about to investigate. There's also the Hachifukushin Circle. Those guys are suspicious, too. Anyway, if I find something else out, I'll make a note in my memories. Bye."

The screen went blank. The memory replay ended.

Performance complete.

I opened my eyes and looked down at the card Moritsuka had left me.

He'd left me two… no, three hints.

"FM radio…" I whispered one of the last things he'd said. "What's that?" I asked the detectives.

"You seriously don't know?" Kozaki was astonished.

"I'm sorry. I've only lived in Japan for a year."

"Kids these days don't listen to the radio, huh? Well, I guess I only listen to it in the car, though."

"What's FM?"

"I think it's the type of frequency or something… What's this about a radio?"

"FM-KCZ in Kichijoji. Ever heard of a mini-FM radio station with that name?"

"Nope. Never."

The two of them glanced at each other and thought. It seemed they really didn't remember.

I took out my phone from my pocket and ran a search online.

The first hit was for a homepage with an old design. It wasn't a homepage for FM-KCZ itself, but rather a list of mini-FM radio stations all across eastern Japan. One of those stations was FM-KCZ.

According to the page, it was privately run by one person, and the station broadcasted news about events in Kichijoji and introductions to local stores. However, it said, the station had been dormant for years. The reason was written on the page.

The host and operator passed away, so the broadcasts stopped.

Death. Again. But what did an FM radio station that stopped broadcasting years ago have to do with anything?

I explained what I'd found about FM-KCZ to Kozaki and Shinoyama and told them that Moritsuka had been researching it. The two of them just looked suspicious.

"We don't have any men to spare right now." They'd said it before I could ask. I'd have to look into it myself.

I picked up my other clue, the manga, again. At the back of the book, Ririka Nishizono was listed as the author, and under her name was an email address and the name of the publishing company.

"It seems someone named Ririka Nishizono is the author of this book." I glanced at the detectives. From the way they were frowning, it seemed unlikely that they'd look into it.

It was hard to call this cooperative. They'd just said they needed all the help they could get, but it seemed they had no intention of helping me.

Feeling like this was a little unfair, I opened my phone and called Oliver. He picked up on the first ring.

"Learn anything?"

"I want you to look into someone for me. Ririka Nishizono. She's using a free email address, it looks like."

"Who is she?"

"Someone Moritsuka was looking into."

"Give me the address."

"All right."

I read him the email address off the last page of the manga. It was a commonly used free email service, but if he tracked it, he might be able to find a phone number.

"Wait five minutes," he said, then hung up without waiting for my answer.

My heart started beating a little faster. It was probably because I'd used my psychometry twice in such a short time.

"May I sit?" I asked, pointing to a chair.

"S-sure. You don't look so good. You okay?"

"Don't worry about me. I'm just a little tired." I sat down on the chair. I sighed a little and used my fingers to wipe the sweat off my forehead. "I'm sorry, can you at least look up the address for FM-KCZ? I'll do the rest of the work myself."

"I don't know if we can use resources on something that's not connected to the case…"

They were still hesitant. Fine, then.

I touched both of their hands at once.

"H-hey, what are you doing?"

It seemed that even a big, tough policeman blushed when he was touched by a high school girl, but I wasn't trying to seduce them.

Begin the performance.

I started with a vision of Shinoyama. Important incidents in his life flashed by on the screen. I chose a few of the most obvious. Then I did the same thing for Kozaki.

"Kozaki, you went to a batting center on Sunday two weeks ago, didn't you? While you were there, you hurt your right hand. Does it still hurt? You think you may have fractured it. I think you should go to a hospital."

"What?!"

"And Shinoyama, you should make up with your wife as soon as possible, okay? This is your third big fight this year, right? Also, you had thirteen cigarettes yesterday, didn't you? You were warned during your last physical that you were smoking too much, so you'd been limiting yourself to ten a day. But yesterday, after what happened with Moritsuka, you smoked three more than usual. Am I wrong?"

"H-how did you know…"

I needed both of them to understand that my psychometry worked, and I needed them to tell the rest of the station that Asuna Kizaki was the real thing.

"This is an official request for help from the FBI. Local information is most easily found by local police. So I want your help."

"R-right."

Shinoyama and Kozaki left the room, both looking confused.

Once they were gone, I took a minute to catch my breath and let my heart rate calm down. If just a few attempts at psychometry in a row were doing this to me, I was going to have a bad time soon. Using my powers was definitely shortening my lifespan, but if I didn't use them now, I wouldn't be able to find what Moritsuka was researching.

A call came in on my phone. The caller was unidentified, but it was probably Oliver.

"Yes, this is Kizaki."

"Ririka Nishizono. A student at Seimei University. I'll email you her address, phone, and social networking accounts. The rest of the information will take some time."

"Thank you."

"Until last month, she was using her email at least once a day, but for the past several days there's no record of her logging in."

"I see." I was curious, but since neither of us could do anything but make guesses right now, I didn't ask.

I decided to ask for something else instead. "Please look into a group called the Hachifukushin Circle as well."

"Something else Moritsuka was looking into?"

"Yes."

"Understood. I'll call you as soon as I've got something," he said, and hung up.

A moment later, an email came with Ririka Nishizono's phone number in it. I called. The phone rang, but she wasn't picking up. If she hadn't been using her email for several days, she was probably out of contact. If I wanted to be optimistic, it was possible she was on a trip overseas. Students were out of class this time of year.

I hung up the phone. The conference room was as quiet as a tomb. I had nothing to do until the detectives got back. To be honest, I hadn't expected to get this much information at the start of my investigation. I'd thought things would be harder. It was safe to say that this was thanks to Moritsuka.

Did he leave that message for me assuming that the FBI would send a psychometer, because he was worried about whether he'd survive? Was something that dangerous hidden within the case he was researching?

I read back through Ririka Nishizono's doujin manga. It was awkward looking at the detailed depictions of men embracing one another.

"Ugh." Each new page introduced me to a world I'd never seen before. I started to feel dizzy.

I didn't have a problem with homosexuality, as long as both people involved were happy, but how much demand was there in Japan for pictures of men having sex like this? Who was the target market, anyway? Men? Women? I had no idea. Where did Moritsuka find this book, anyway?

"Huh?" Suddenly, my eyes landed on one of the panels.

It was the second story in a collection of five stories. There was a box there that the manga identified as the "Kotoribako." Unlike the characters in the manga, this drawing was detailed, as if the artist had been looking at it while she drew it.

At first I thought there was a pattern drawn on the surface of the box, but then I saw that all the lines in the pattern ran from side to side, as if the whole box was made from tiny little pieces of wood.

"A box…"

It reminded me of what Shinoyama had just told me about the murder at Enmeiji temple.

"You could say it's like… Like a book of prophecy," Moritsuka had said in his memories about the box.

"A book of prophecy…"

The title on the cover read *The Bottom of the Deep Water*. When I thought about what that meant, a chill ran up my spine.

Moritsuka had died in Inokashira Park in the middle of the night. He'd died at the bottom of deep water, and not alone, but with 255 other people.

It was like the book had foretold that.

I gulped and slammed the manga shut.

The inside and outside of Inokashira Park were very different.

Outside, there were still many signs of life. The media and gawkers were still camping out from morning till night, waiting for some new piece of information.

Everything was different inside the park. Things were returning to their natural state of calm.

There were several heavily-armored cars inside the park that belonged to the Self-Defense Forces. There were over a dozen police officers wandering around the grounds, but they were all in a relaxed and easygoing mode.

Until a few days ago, this place had looked like something out of a natural disaster, but now that seemed like a dream. All the bodies had been dragged up and moved to another location, and the rumor was that the police were going to end their investigation soon.

However, the area around the lake was still covered with blue tarp, and nobody was allowed in. If they had tried to hide what was going on here, there'd be no end of media people trying to sneak in and take photographs.

The sky was still filled with helicopters. I'd gotten used to the noise.

I couldn't help but laugh. This bench was supposed to be off-limits too, but nobody came over to stop me. I could see everyone, but nobody was looking at me. Everyone was treating me like I wasn't there.

Was this how the invisible man felt? No one could see him, but in exchange he could see everyone, in any way he liked.

It felt like I'd been cut off from the world.

No, it wasn't just a feeling. I was dead. I *had* been cut off from the world.

I knew, or thought I knew, how I had died. I'd sunk to the bottom of the deep water here at Inokashira Lake.

I hadn't wanted to die here, but I clearly remembered that moment. My first feeling was…sadness, because I wouldn't get to touch any cute boys anymore.

It was a feeling that didn't matter at all. Of course, it didn't really matter whether I could touch them or not. If I could draw them, that was enough for me.

Now that I was dead, I felt free in a lot of ways. When I was alive, I'd thought that there were many limits on what I could do. Now, I felt so free.

Two men wearing suits, who looked like detectives, passed by me. I'd been watching this park for a while, but the detective I'd seen before, the one in the trench coat who looked like a young boy, had yet to show himself.

The detective in the manga I'd drawn. This was where I'd met him. Sometimes I'd see people in trench coats and hope they were him. I hadn't fallen in love or anything like that, but I did want to talk to him again.

But if I hadn't seen him, maybe he wasn't part of the local station. Or perhaps...

Had he sunk to the bottom of the deep water, too?

"There's no time left! You must act now!"

"Oh?"

I heard a creaky old voice I recognized from the other side of the tarps. I stood up and went outside the tarp.

I looked around and quickly found the source of the voice.

In the middle of the space surrounded by the media and the gawkers, "God" was screaming to no one in particular.

"The experimenters have at last destroyed the samples! You're next!" His voice was creaky but carried far. Nothing had changed since the last time I'd seen him. "Don't think that they're the last! Their conspiracy has only begun! If you don't act now, something terrible will happen!"

It was a desperate message, but everyone was ignoring it. It looked like everyone recognized he was there, unlike how they treated me.

"Nikola Tesla's experiment continues here, now, in Musashino! Two monsters are brainwashing the people, and the masters of the monsters are the enemies of humanity!"

I walked over to God, who was continuing his speech. I got so close that I could almost feel the spittle flying from his mouth. Up close, I saw that his skin was dry from the sun, and parts along his wrinkles seemed to be decaying. His breath was so awful, I thought I'd throw up. He definitely didn't brush his teeth.

It was strange. Even in death, I could still smell things.

"Hello, God. Can you see me?"

God ignored me completely. "The wireless power transmission project is not dead!" He was still screaming, not realizing there was someone right in front of him.

Spittle flew everywhere, but it didn't feel dirty to me. His eyeballs shook a little as they poked out from their deep-set sockets.

He was blind, wasn't he? So even gods went blind. If that was the case, who would it be who found me?

The Lord of Hell?

"The devil's experiment has revived from the pit of death! Disaster will befall not one or two hundred, but all life on Earth! What are you doing? Look with your eyes, and know! Learn of them and their terrible plan!"

It was a shame that God had abandoned me, but I felt a little satisfied. It wouldn't do for God to just answer anybody who asked a question. He'd seem much less mystical. He should be like a little boy, always selfish and only concerned with himself.

"Farewell, God." I gave my goodbyes and walked past the circle of people watching God from a distance.

I went back to the bench where I'd been sitting and opened the sketchbook in my hands, beginning to draw nothing in particular. If I could, I wanted to draw the corpse of a boy that had just floated up from the bottom of the lake.

It would be very cruel, and very sensual.

If only another body would come up from the lake, I wished to myself as I began to draw.

"Even as a ghost, you don't change, huh?"

Suddenly, I heard a voice speaking to me.

I looked up from my sketchbook, a little surprised. "Oh, you're…"

It was the cute little boy I'd met before who had called himself Sagami.

His skin was so white you could almost see through it, and his limbs were so wonderfully delicate that I shivered. I couldn't help but get naughty thoughts. I would have loved to see his corpse.

The boy sat down next to me without asking and began to spread out a series of brightly colored cards on his lap. I took a moment to enjoy the contrast they made against his white skin as I began to resume my drawing.

The boy looked at me as if challenging me. "You're boring, aren't you?"

"Am I? You always look like you're having fun, don't you?"

"I'm not like normal people. That's why."

"I see."

His innocent arrogance was so cute.

"I really am amazing. I'm one of the chosen people!"

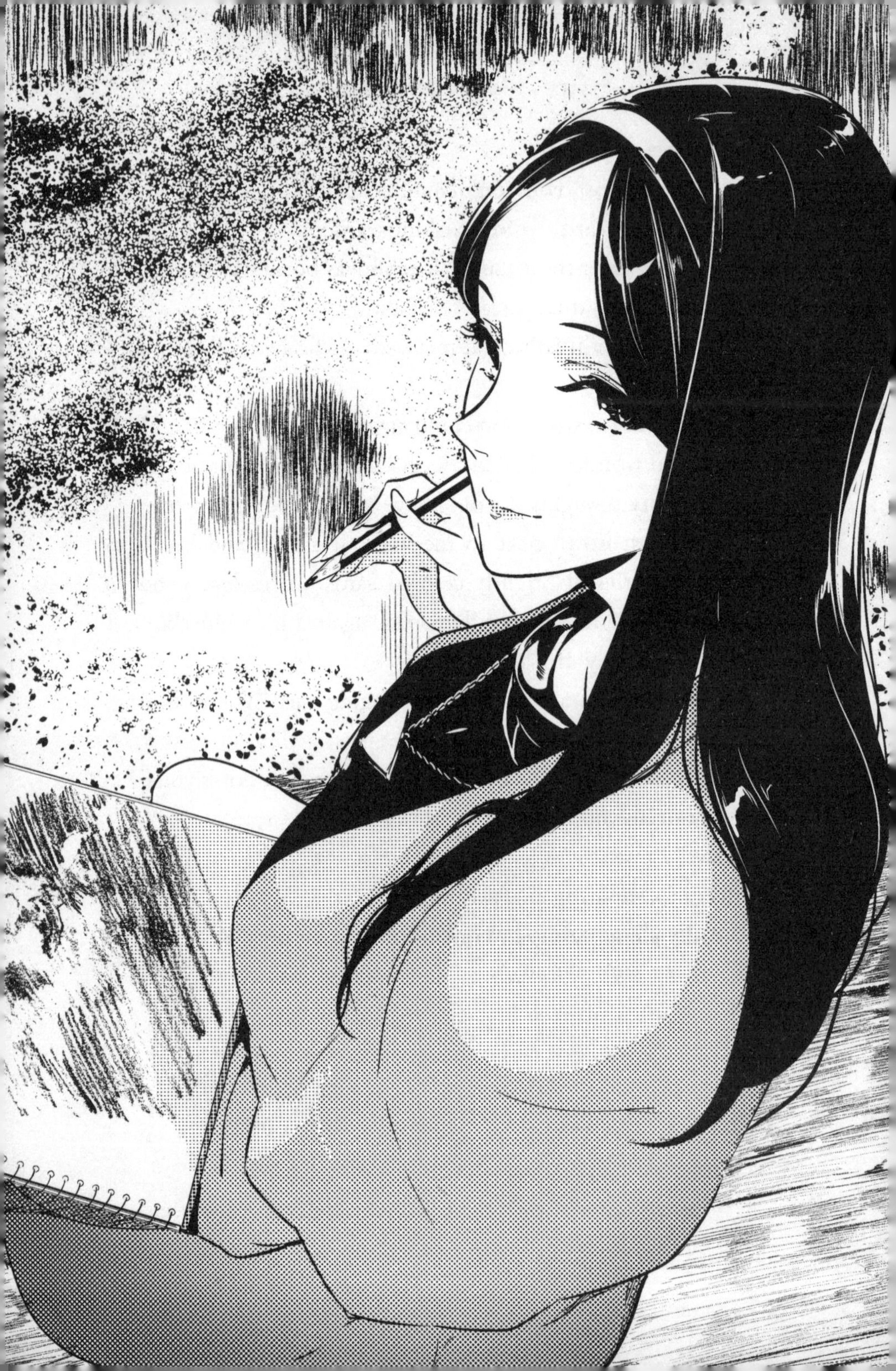

"The chosen people?" I stopped my sketching as I heard these unfamiliar words. The boy must have been pleased with my reaction, because he grinned and continued.

"I was a winner from the moment I was born. My parents are super rich, so I got this special treatment."

"What kind of treatment?"

"I don't die."

"What a coincidence. I'm immortal, too."

After all, I was already dead. I'd never heard of any creature dying twice. Now that I was already dead, I would probably never die.

"It's not like being a ghost. No, maybe it is? Do you know what scandium is? Well, I'm sure you don't. But if you inject yourself with it, you can go on living even if you die."

"A ghost, huh?"

"Then we are the same."

The boy and I looked at each other and exchanged a smile.

Scandium. A word I'd never heard before. If what the boy was saying was true, was that flowing through my veins right now?

"How do you get it?"

"They sell it."

"At the pharmacy?"

"No way. At a place called the Hachifukushin Circle."

"Can I get some, too?"

"No way. You have to be chosen, like me."

"That's a shame," I said, hoping to make the boy feel special. "Then you're a ghost now?"

"No, no. Were you listening? I'm alive."

Hmm. So right now, we were communicating between the

living and the dead.

"I died in that lake, you know," I said.

"So what?"

"Remember what you said? That I was a ghost. If you can see me, doesn't that mean it's natural to think that you're a ghost, too?"

The boy's eyes went wide as if he was surprised. He hadn't thought of that, it seemed.

"But you're alive, and you can see and talk to ghosts. Amazing, huh?"

The boy fell silent. I wanted to kiss him all over his pouty face.

"Hey, is it rough being able to see ghosts?"

"Rough?"

"I mean, there's a lot more people who have died in the past than are alive now, right? So shouldn't the town be filled with dead people? What kind of people do you see? Samurai? Soldiers?" I asked, being deliberately mean.

I smiled softly and spoke in a gentle voice. I wanted to tease him.

"Is that poor girl you stuffed into the Kotoribako standing right next to you, glaring at you angrily?"

"There's nothing like that."

"I see. How boring. It's a shame, since you can see me." The boy stared at me. I glanced at him and returned to my sketching.

Inokashira Park was busier than it usually was. The boy said he was alive, but the media on the other side of the blue tarp were ignoring him just like they were ignoring me. He sat next to me, tilting his head to the left and right as he whispered to himself.

"So there are some ghosts you can see, and some you can't. What does that mean?"

It seemed so easy.

Go to Musashino Police Station and ask where the bodies from the Inokashira Lake incident were being kept. That was all I had to do.

"A member of my family was on the list of victims. I want to identify them. Please tell me where they are."

That was all I had to say. I couldn't think of a reason why they'd refuse.

But...

When I went to Musashino Station, nobody I talked to would answer me.

Nobody heard me. They ignored me like I wasn't even there. All I ended up doing was reinforcing the theory that I was dead.

Even in this state, there were probably other ways to get information. I could use the phone, it seemed, so I could pretend to be a family member and call the station. Or maybe I could use my dad's connections in the media to find out, if I had to.

However, I felt like if I didn't put it off until tomorrow, I wasn't going to last. I was more tired than I thought I was. I started to think about whether it was due to psychological exhaustion or because I was dead, and I stopped.

There was no point in thought experiments like those.

In the end, by the time I got back home, I was exhausted. When I got inside, my mom was sitting in the middle of the living room on the first floor. All the lights were off.

She looked like she'd aged even more over the last few days. It hurt to see her like that. I wanted to talk to her, but I already knew she couldn't hear me.

I fled up to the second floor. My father's study was a mess, with the notes I'd written and my father's books scattered all over the floor. I'd locked myself in the room and worked on decoding the list. I knew I had to clean it up, but right now I didn't feel like it.

I looked up at the ceiling again. The countless dots there were a list of the 256 names. At this point, there was no point to the list… maybe. I didn't want to admit it, but the more time passed, the more the names on the list and the victims matched up.

"Maybe my name is here, too…" I shook my head to drive the cold I suddenly felt away.

"Dad. The research you poured your life into is being called a conspiracy by people who don't have any scientific evidence at all."

I'd been one of them, once. Right now, I didn't know if my dad was right or not, but I *did* have the list. It was clear that my dad knew something. That's why I wanted to talk to my dad now, to reveal the truth.

Of course, if I really was a ghost, then maybe Dad was out there somewhere, and I could talk to him.

How stupid. Was I starting to believe in the occult, too?

"Where'd my dad get this list, anyway? And who was he hoping would find it?"

It didn't do anybody any good hidden here, especially now that the incident was over. Did my dad die trying to protect this thing?

"The only time people get killed for conspiracies is in fiction. Or did he want to leave this riddle so someone could solve it? Why go through all the trouble? Did he want to be the hero of some tragic play or something?"

I thought he was more intelligent than that. He was more like a character in a third-rate novel. Did he understand how frustrating this was?

"Come on, Dad. It's not fair for me to be the only one talking here. Come on out and prove it. Prove I'm wrong. This time, I'll prove all of your ridiculous theories…wrong."

Damn it.

I bit my lip and left the study. The fact that I was letting emotions like these threaten to crush me made me want to vomit.

After spending so much time with Gamon, Aikawa, and Miss Sumikaze, maybe I'd started to change. Or maybe now that I was just static particles with no body, that was having an effect on me. There was also the possibility that I wasn't me anymore, just another, similar personality. Maybe I just hadn't noticed it.

"Even thinking that is a stupid conspiracy theory."

I went to my room and collapsed on the bed. Usually my mattress creaked, but today it didn't.

PARANORMAL SCIENCE NVL
Occultic;Nine
オカルティック・ナイン

THERE IS NO SUCH THING AS THE "OCCULT." IT CAN ALL BE DISPROVED BY SCIENCE.
ONLY THOSE WHO HAVE ACCEPTED EVERYTHING
HAVE THE RIGHT TO KNOW THE TRUTH.

▶ site 63: Yuta Gamon

When I went through the gate, the school seemed quieter than usual.

I'd gone into town and headed for the school. It wasn't a place I particularly liked. I hadn't been here since Dr. Hashigami's murder, for one thing. So why had I come here now? I didn't know.

I looked into the teachers' office, a little nervously. Even though it was Saturday, almost all of the teachers were there. They were talking about something with serious looks on their faces. The air in the room felt depressing.

"Excuse me." I went into the room, but nobody noticed me.

Yeah, that's just what I'd expected. That still didn't prove I was dead. It would feel a lot more realistic if it turned out that I was just invisible. So no matter how much the teachers ignored me, it didn't bother me.

I looked around the room and saw a whiteboard behind the head teacher's desk. It had a list of more than ten names of students and their classes.

"Were you able to get a hold of Akanishi's family?"

"No, not yet."

"Where are they, and what the hell are they doing?"

"Sir, the parents of the new students are asking when school's going to begin!"

"Hello, this is Seimei Academy High School."

The phones were ringing, and the teachers were running around and shouting. There was a lot of chaos. That would explain why nobody was paying any attention to me.

I decided to try talking to Mr. Abekawa, my language teacher, who was right by me. "Um, Mr. Abekawa?"

His shoulders were slumped, and he was staring at a list of student names and addresses. His hands shook as he held it.

"Hello? Sir?"

He didn't seem to hear me. Well, he was getting a little old. Maybe he was going deaf.

I looked back at the whiteboard. There were dozens of names on the list. One of them was mine.

Yeah, saw that coming. I wasn't going to let it surprise me, though!

"Oh…"

Miyuu Aikawa.

Myu-Pom's name was there, too… Hmm… then what about Ryotasu?

I looked at each name on the whiteboard. "It's not there…"

Ryotasu's name wasn't there. What did that mean?

"Hahaha! It means nothing! It doesn't matter! I'm gonna have a great time with this ghost thing—oh, invisible-man thing—or maybe out-of-body-experience thing? Whatever it is, I'm off to have a great time!" I forced myself to laugh and left the room.

I decided to head to the AV room next.

This was where Myu-Pom used to do her fortune-telling, but now there was no one here. I looked in my classroom too, but of course nobody was there either.

Man, this was boring. It was so boring I had to yawn. School was really boring, so I decided not to use it for my affiliate blog.

I left the school and headed towards the station, but suddenly noticed something strange.

"Why's everything so empty?"

I hadn't noticed this morning, but today the shopping street in front of Kichijoji Station was surprisingly empty.

This was because of the 256 Incident, right? Or maybe it was just everything that had been happening in Kichijoji lately.

Nobody who didn't live in this neighborhood would want to come here, unless they were some kind of weirdo or seriously into the occult.

I thought about this as I walked, and then a middle-aged man almost ran right into me.

"Hey!" I quickly dodged before I slammed into him, but he didn't even try to move away.

He was totally going to slam into me. Was this some new type of scam? He just looked like an ordinary old man, and he didn't come try to shake me down after he almost hit me. He just ignored me as he walked right by.

It was like he didn't even see me.

"Maybe I really am an invisible man."

The same thing happened two or three more times. There were barely any people, even in front of the station, so if someone was watching where they were going—or even if they were buried in their phone—there was no way they could collide with someone. Yet people kept doing it anyway.

The first was a serious-looking middle school student; the second, a woman in her twenties in a pretty dress. I thought it might be okay to slam into the girl, but when we got close I dodged out of reflex. She didn't apologize at all.

I got a little annoyed and stood where the most people were, though it was still far emptier than usual. Before even a minute had passed, one of a pair of young men almost rammed into me. After dodging at the last second, I chased after the man.

"H-hey! A-a-apolo…"

"What?"

"I'm sorry."

He glared at me so angrily that I apologized, but the way he was acting was weird. His look quickly turned to one of surprise as he looked around him. He didn't look at me.

"Something wrong?"

"Oh, no…huh?"

He turned back to the other man he was with in confusion, and then they both went down Harmonica Alley as if I wasn't even there.

He was the fourth person to respond to my voice. The number of people who'd ignored me was over three times that. Even when people did respond, they treated me like I was the invisible man.

"Come on, why are you all pretending you can't see me? I'm

right here! I can get run over by cars!"

I ran out into the road and smacked right into the side mirror of a passing car. An awful pain ran down my arm. It was so bad I dropped to my knees right there on the street.

"S-see? I can hit things! I'm not a ghost! Oww… that hurt."

I wasn't sure if I was happy or in pain, but I was crying either way.

Man, that really hurt. Maybe I broke my arm. The car had kept going after it hit me. That was totally a hit and run.

A crime.

I was right in front of the station, so a bunch of people should've seen me, but nobody came running up or said anything. What was going on here? Was Japan just done for as a nation?

"Somebody call the cops! There was a hit and run! Call an ambulance!" I cried, but nobody near the station responded.

I started to cry. It felt like the whole world was bullying me.

"Oh, so that's how it is? Everybody's ignoring me, huh? Yeah, cause I'm dead! Sorry!"

I went to roll on the ground, but doing it in the street was a little too scary, so I moved over towards the station's turnstiles and laid out on the ground.

Nobody would notice me here. Nobody would say anything. So I was going to just do whatever I felt like.

The pain in my arm got a little better. I was glad to see it wasn't broken.

"Haha… nobody can see me… LOL."

Just then…

"Huh?"

A woman in a skirt walked right over me.

I gasped.

I-I saw it.

I saw what was up her skirt.

"I saw it! It was pink!"

Oh no! I was going to be arrested for peeping! I quickly stood up and tried to think of an excuse, but she ignored me and quickly walked into the station.

The people around me ignored me as well. Nobody even looked at me.

"Hahah. This is great. I-I think I've finally found the greatest possible story for my blog!"

The internet was all about sex and violence, and the more sensational the story, the better. It didn't matter who died or who said what, as long as you got the page views. That meant I had to use the situation I was in to the best of my advantage!

I looked around. There were three teenage girls standing in front of the bus stop. It was still March, and still cold, but their bare legs were exposed under their short skirts.

I walked over to the three of them and crouched down to look under their skirts.

"Right! White! Black shorts! Blue!"

Nobody said anything. The girls didn't even notice me.

"Hahaha, this is great! This is great! Being a ghost is awesome! It's so simple that it doesn't make me feel anything, though. Also, Girl B! In the black shorts! You're blaspheming the very idea of being a teenage girl! You've shortened your skirt, but you're still wearing shorts to keep anybody from seeing anything? Don't you have any pride?"

The three girls didn't respond.

They say that the greater the effort something requires, the greater the payoff. In that sense, seeing their panties did nothing for me at all. It felt like looking at the panties on an anime figure. Sure, it felt a little immoral, but it wasn't sexually exciting at all. Still, it was kind of fun to be able to see something I didn't normally get to see.

"If it's this easy, just looking at panties isn't enough."

As a blogger, I needed to push things to their limits. It was something that only I could do now, after all.

For instance, maybe I could sneak into a cute girl's house. Or maybe go to a girl's school and see what kinds of naughty things they got up to there. Or...

"Oh!"

Come to think of it, there was an old bathhouse just a few minutes away from here!

My body shook a little at the boldness of what I was about to do. But in a sense, it was something every man had dreamed of. Every man, right?

If this worked, my ghost liveblogging at Kirikiri Basara would get some amazing view numbers! Plus, maybe there were other people who were ghosts besides me that were in trouble? As an occult blogger, it was my job to tell them what was safe and what wasn't. Looking up a girl's skirt in public had made me really bold, so I walked straight over to the bathhouse.

The bathhouse was in a residential area in Kichijoji. It wasn't one of the super bathhouses that were so popular now; it was an old, beat-up building.

It was still evening, but the sign was already up. They were open. If it hadn't opened yet, I would've had to go to Mitaka or Ogikubo, so I was pretty lucky.

"Alright...this is Snake. I'm about to begin my infiltration. *Bzzzt...bzzzt.*" I went in, deliberately not taking my shoes off. I walked past the counter and went into the room with the red awning marked "Ladies."

It was my first time going into a women's bath, so my feet were shaking with nervousness. I tried my best to calm myself down. Nobody was going to see me. There was no need to worry about a thing. I knew that, but still I couldn't help feeling a little afraid.

I went in quietly, even though I didn't need to.

There was nobody there. There weren't any girls changing. That made sense. Very few people were taking a bath at this hour, especially with so few people out on the streets of Kichijoji.

I was a little disappointed, and then I saw a flash of movement at the back. Someone was here! There was a girl here! I gulped. I thought I'd break into a grin, but I didn't.

I felt like a spy on a secret mission. I couldn't afford to screw up. I didn't have time to grin. I was completely serious. Even if I was cheating and playing in god mode, I couldn't let my guard down.

I stalked towards the door that led to the baths, but then...

The door opened, and out from the baths and into the changing room came a wrinkly old granny.

For some reason, I felt like coughing.

This was bad. The tension was starting to evaporate, and the mood was ruined. I could feel myself beginning to reconsider this whole thing.

I closed my eyes and tried to imagine a harem of young naked girls like I'd always seen in manga and anime.

Yes, that was what I wanted!

Sorry, old lady, but I'm not here for you! I passed by her and headed for the bath, trying my best not to look at her, and then I opened my eyes wide.

"What?"

It was empty.

There were only two customers in the whole bath, and one of them was another wrinkly grandma. She was floating in the tub and sighing like an old man.

Ugh.

What was this? Was this reality?

I almost wept tears of frustration as my eyes turned towards the other customer. "Oh…"

She had her back to me as she scrubbed herself, rubbing hard with a bubble-covered cloth. She was young. She had the body of a teenager or someone in her twenties. If nothing else, she wasn't an old lady.

She was a little big-boned, but her body was toned and healthy. The curves of her waist and butt weren't much different from any moe anime character. In a sense, it was artistic. Her shoulders were broad, and the muscles on her arms were thick. She looked like someone who worked out.

I was so happy that there was a young woman here. God hadn't abandoned me.

Thank you, God. Now Kirikiri Basara will survive.

I let out a little cheer, then turned toward the girl.

"Huh?"

"Huh?"

Our eyes met.

She was pretty cute. Was she in college? She looked a little older than me. There were small bags under her eyes.

Huh? Wait, why did our eyes meet? How?

I panicked a little as her eyes went wide with surprise.

Don't tell me... She could see me?!

"Kyaaaah!" Her scream echoed throughout the bath. "Pervert! Peeping tom!" She pointed at me and screamed.

"You can see me?! You can see me?!"

"Somebody call the police!"

No way! I thought nobody could see me! Or was she already dead, too? Wait, there wasn't time to think about that!

I quickly ran out of the women's bath.

"*Hahh...hahh...* I can't believe someone saw me."

I'd run a good long while without even thinking about the direction I was heading. The next thing I knew, I was under the raised pedestrian bridge along Kichijoji Street, which ran right through Inokashira.

I panted as I wiped the sweat pouring off my forehead with my sleeve. It seemed strangely quiet. Everybody probably wanted to stay away from Inokashira. There were cars, but no pedestrians.

Man, that scared me. It was just like when I picked up the pass case. There was someone in that bathhouse who could see me and react to me.

Wait, there were only three people there. What were the odds that one of them could see me? I had the worst luck. Because of that, I'd missed my chance to see that healthy, gym-going girl's breasts! What a shame! I guess the world wasn't that nice of a place. I'd thought I was in god mode, but I wasn't at all.

"Did she die in the 256 Incident, too?"

Or was she somebody with a strong spirit sense, like Toko had said? Either way, I was exhausted. I didn't have the energy to go back into that bath again. Actually, even if nobody had seen me, I probably wouldn't have had the energy left. Going into that bath had drained a lot out of me. I'd thought about trying to at least have a little fun, but evidently that wasn't going to happen.

"If this is a dream, let me wake up!"

If this was a dream, like Sarai said, then maybe I'd wake up soon, right? To be honest, I was feeling really lonely being ignored all the time.

Suddenly, there was a voice from the Skysensor. "So go find out for sure, you pervert!"

It was so sudden I thought the girl had followed me from the baths, and I tried to run. I tripped and fell to the ground.

"What are you doing? You're so dense."

"Z-Zonko?! Is that you?!"

"You're making too many excuses! And you're playing around too much!"

"Zonko, why haven't you said anything? Why didn't you answer me?"

"There's no law that says I have to answer you every time you say something. I'm actually really busy."

"That's so selfish. You just said all that important-sounding stuff and left. How could you do that to me?"

"Yeah, yeah. Let's go."

"Huh? Go where?"

"You want to know if you're alive or not, right? So the fastest way is to look at your own body, right?"

My own…body…

Sarai and Toko had said that that was our top priority.

"But…where is my body?"

"Daiseiji," Zonko said calmly. "That's where they're keeping the bodies."

That was the temple next to Inokashira, right? It was pretty big, so maybe it was a good place to keep 256 bodies.

"Your body's there, too."

"My body is there…"

Then I really was dead?

"Zonko, is there a chance you're lying? And wait, how do you know this?"

"All you have to do is ask the police. There are so many unidentified bodies that the police are actually asking for information."

I stared at the Skysensor skeptically.

"You don't want to just stay ignorant forever, right?"

Maybe, but I wished she wouldn't make going to see your body sound so simple. I didn't have any other options, though, so in the end I would go.

"Why are you always so selfish? You never give me time to prepare!" I said. "Huh? Zonko?"

The Skysensor had gone silent again.

"Oh, jeez! Damn it!"

I was so mad that I wanted to punch the Skysensor, but it was so important to me that I managed to just barely control myself.

PARANORMAL SCIENCE NVL

Occultic;Nine

オカルティック・ナイン

THERE IS NO SUCH THING AS THE "OCCULT." IT CAN ALL BE DISPROVED BY SCIENCE.
ONLY THOSE WHO HAVE ACCEPTED EVERYTHING
HAVE THE RIGHT TO KNOW THE TRUTH.

▶ site 64: Shun Moritsuka

"Oh man, oh man. This was a mistake," I said into the phone as I entered Kichijoji Park in the middle of the night. Kichijoji was even quieter at night than it was during the day. A bunch of the stores that were normally open late had closed early. "I still can't believe I was on the list of the 256. Their information network is really something."

"You screwed up, Agent Moritsuka."

"Yeah, I sure did. Sorry."

"Apologies are unnecessary."

"I'm sure." I carefully walked up the steps of a small slide, the phone still in one hand. Maybe one good thing about being a ghost was that I could play on children's playground equipment without having to worry about anybody seeing me.

"You're sure it doesn't feel like you're dead?"

"Not in the least. That's why I was so surprised when I got the call."

When I got to the top of the slide, I took out a can of coffee I'd put in my coat pocket. It was hot; I'd just bought it a second ago from a vending machine. It was too hot to hold, in fact, so I'd put it in my pocket to cool it down.

I put my phone between my jaw and my shoulder and opened the pull tab with both hands. I took a sip, and surprisingly, it was warm. "Really, how the hell does this phone work anyway? Should I add that to the list of things to investigate?"

"There's no time now."

"That's a shame. It might be the invention of the century. You could call it 'the Ghost Phone' and sell it for a billion dollars."

Actually, I had an idea about how this phone worked. That's why I was able to guess that the call would cut off soon, and as if to prove me right, the voice was starting to get faint and covered with static.

"Well, if I'm dead, I'm dead. I would've hoped for a cooler way to die, but that's just me. Like I tracked down the criminal and he got me at the last minute, or something like that."

"What will you do now?"

My joke was completely ignored.

"Inspector Zenigata, whom I respect greatly, would've made it look like he was dead and then come back to life three minutes before the end of the anime. But I think it'll be difficult for me to do that. Since I'm dead, I was able to take a long vacation, so I'm going back to working on the investigation. It may all be for nothing, though."

"I see."

"We can assume this call is being monitored, so this will be the last time I talk to you. 'El Psy Kongroo,' and all that."

"What?"

"It was a phrase from an anime a few years ago. Oh, maybe it was a game?"

"Good luck." The voice on the other end of the line seemed to be shaking a little. I couldn't tell if it was some emotion they were feeling or just due to the static. Knowing their personality, they weren't the type to feel sad about my death. Maybe they were scared to be talking to a dead man.

"By the way, who's taking over for me?"

"Her. You know her well, right? She's already started work—"

"Did you not understand why I had her removed a year ago?"

They didn't answer. The connection was dead.

I shrugged and gulped down the rest of the coffee. I tossed the empty can at a trash can a good distance away. It flew in a beautiful arc, like in an anime—and then disappeared into the darkness before it landed. It didn't do anything romantic, like turn into particles of light. It just vanished without a sound.

"I think, therefore I am, huh? This reminds me of Descartes."

Where do people go when they die?

That question had been unanswered since the dawn of the very idea of philosophy. Did I know the answer now? As I wondered, I felt someone looking at me and turned my eyes towards the front of the park.

There was a man standing beneath the streetlight, alone. He was a tall man, dressed all in black, the kind of person who would surely be questioned by the police if he was out late at night.

"Did you wait for me to get off the phone?" I asked, but the man didn't answer. "I didn't think you'd actually come. Do you like me, perhaps?"

The man ignored my joke, too.

"Maybe I should introduce myself, devil? No, perhaps…"

I went down the slide and walked over to the man. There was quite a difference in our heights. I had to look up at him. God was very unfair. "Or perhaps it would be better to use your real name: Kiryu Kusakabe."

The eyes of the man—Kiryu Kusakabe—narrowed as if he were feeling cautious.

I'd looked him up once I'd started researching the Black Magic Agency, and I'd found he had quite the resume.

"I've done a lot of looking into you. There are a lot of people in the police like me, with too much time on their hands."

"Hmph. All that work, and you ended up dead. That's pretty funny."

Ooh, sharp tongue! But it would take more than that to provoke me.

"You're pretty happy I'm dead though, aren't you? Now I can't do anything to Aria. Or rather, Ria Minase. Oh, but she's also—"

"How much do you know?" Kusakabe glared at me. The light in his eyes was incredibly fierce. Even in the darkness, I could tell he wanted to kill me. Scary!

"I actually don't know all that much. I don't even know where the professor's hair went. Do you?"

He continued to glare. Well, even if he did know, he wouldn't tell me. Time for my next move, then.

"I'll tell you one thing I do know—three years ago…"

Before I could say anything else, I heard the sound of him

gritting his teeth hard.

"…After an explosion at a fuel battery factory, you gained the ability to leave your own body." I watched for his response.

Kusakabe silently put a cigarette in his mouth and lit it. Was he unconcerned, or trying to hide his fear?

"Three years ago, you were hit with a huge amount of scandium. That's what gave you the power to leave your body." I went over to a nearby bench and sat down. "That factory was dealing with new kinds of alpha-type scandium isotopes. Think you could tell me more about them? How about it?"

When I looked back at him, he was gone. He'd vanished without a sound.

Oh dear, I guess he'd left. What a shame.

"Don't get too deep into this, devil."

PARANORMAL SCIENCE NVL

Occultic;Nine

オカルティック・ナイン

THERE IS NO SUCH THING AS THE "OCCULT." IT CAN ALL BE DISPROVED BY SCIENCE.
ONLY THOSE WHO HAVE ACCEPTED EVERYTHING
HAVE THE RIGHT TO KNOW THE TRUTH.

▶ site 65: Asuna Kizaki

Daiseiji Temple was a big temple right near Inokashira Park, surrounded by white stone walls. It was built as a shrine to the god Yakushi Nyorai, and it was a very solemn place.

The police were going in and out of it, looking busy. Outside the gate, the media had set up camp. The main shrine had a "No Admittance" sign on the door. Cold white smoke poured out from within. It was probably dry ice, used to delay the decay of the bodies.

The building held the bodies of over two hundred people dragged up from the bottom of Inokashira Lake. Of course, Moritsuka was in here, too.

I'd ridden over from the dorm on my bike, but I wasn't sure if it was okay to go inside, so I simply stood there. Just then, Shinoyama came out from the building, and our eyes met. He waved at me.

"You came, huh? This way."

I moved my bike off to the side so it wouldn't get in the way, then followed him inside.

The floor was covered with a plastic sheet. There were large clumps of dry ice here and there all over the floor, and it was freezing cold despite being spring. The massive temple building was gloomy even now in the daytime, and I shivered from the chill.

There were rows of simply constructed coffins. When I saw that each one of them held a body, I was stunned by the sheer number. There were probably more dead people than living ones here now.

I couldn't look away from it. No matter which way I turned, there were coffins.

I was an FBI agent, whether I looked like it or not, and I'd seen bodies before. Each time I had, I'd done my best to avoid thinking of them as human. Otherwise, I'd get too emotional and wouldn't be able to do my investigation properly.

In all those cases, though, the bodies had been in awful shape, so while it had been shocking, it was easy to tell myself that these were just things, not people. This time, however, none of the bodies were badly damaged. They were all in pristine condition. There was far too much left of how they'd looked when they were alive.

Would I be able to control myself when I saw Moritsuka's body? I got a little scared thinking about it.

"Moritsuka's this way." Shinoyama guided me towards the back.

Just like the documents I'd read had said, the 256 corpses were of all different genders and ages. There were adults, and five-year-old children. It seemed like half were men and half were women.

Suddenly, I heard a woman sobbing in the quiet temple. She was in her thirties, and she was clinging to one of the coffins and crying. Next to her was a boy who looked like he was in elementary school. He just stood there in shock. They must have been one of the families.

My chest started to tighten.

Shinoyama came to a stop in front of the coffins. "This is Moritsuka," he said hesitantly, pointing to the coffin in front of him.

It had been a long time since I'd seen Moritsuka's face, but he hadn't changed much at all. He looked so peaceful, like at any moment he might open his eyes and say, "Hey, how've you been?"

"It's like he's asleep, isn't it?"

Shinoyama didn't answer, but instead said flatly, "We haven't finished going over all the victims yet, but Moritsuka definitely died of drowning."

Drowning...

I'd read about the cause of death in the documents I'd been given, but after coming here, I was starting to wonder more about it.

Many of the corpses here hadn't swollen up because the temperature in the lake was cold in February and they were found quickly. But their expressions were so peaceful, and there were no signs of the suffering that drowning victims usually experienced.

Were they all drugged and unconscious when it happened? But several of the bodies had been examined, and no trace of drugs had been found...

There was no point in thinking about it. I'd just do what I came here to do.

"Let me see Moritsuka's things," I said.

Shinoyama pointed towards a plastic container next to the coffin. There was barely anything inside. Just a few waterlogged trading cards and some receipts. It would be hard to get anything useful out of them.

"Is this all?"

"It's not just Moritsuka. It's the same for all of them. Far too few of them are carrying anything that would help ID them."

"Is that why it's taking so long to identify them?"

"Yeah," Shinoyama grunted and nodded.

I dropped to my knees on the cold floor and looked at Moritsuka up close.

Really, his face was so peaceful. There was no sign of the suffering that occurs when water enters your lungs. Was it possible that someone who had drowned himself could look like that?

If he'd died without suffering, then at least that was fortunate, maybe.

"I'm sorry." I gulped, took off my glove, and put my hand against Moritsuka's forehead. His skin was cool to the touch. It was so cold I almost cried.

No.

This wasn't the time to let my emotions take control. If I didn't stay on top of things, Moritsuka would scold me.

I closed off my feelings, shut my eyes, and focused.

Begin the performance.

I decided to go back to twenty minutes before his death.

A street, lit up by streetlights.

I knew the place: it was Kichijoji Street. It was late at night, and Moritsuka was walking at a regular rhythm. He didn't seem to be in a hurry. He went from the road into the park, and even though it was late at night, there were many people there. All of them were walking silently towards the lake.

There was no hesitation at all in anyone's steps. Their movements were swift and certain. Nobody was stopping, and nobody seemed to be there against their will.

Adults, kids, men, women—they were all acting as if they were out for a walk, but it was the middle of the night. It wasn't an hour when that many people would go for a walk.

Eventually, they all reached the shrine to Benzaiten that was next to the lake. The adults climbed over the small fence separating it from the lake, and the children went under it.

Nobody spoke. They were all completely silent.

It wasn't a deep lake. Even a child would only be chest-deep in the water if he stood up.

Like they were getting into the bath or swimming in a pool, they went out to the center of the lake and crouched, sinking of their own will into the water.

A line formed. They weren't going over the fence one by one, but one group would go out and sink, and then the next group would follow.

Moritsuka was no different. He walked out into the middle of the lake like it was the most normal thing in the world and sank down in the water. His body collided with one of the others who had already sunk, and he looked up from the bottom of the lake towards the surface.

You could see the moonlight on the lake's surface. The waves formed by all the people entering the water made the moonlight seem to waver. But his view was quickly blocked out by the next victim who came after him...

"What is this?"

I forced the memory to come to an end.

I'd been able to replay his memories. I'd heard the sound of him stepping on the dried leaves, the sound of him falling into the water, but I hadn't heard any voices.

It wasn't just spoken words. With my psychometry, I could hear the internal voices of the dead. This time, though, I'd heard nothing at all. There was no strong desire to end it all, no sense of relief at escaping into death, no reason to die, no emotions driving him toward death…

No fear of death, even. There was nothing at all. Nothing but emptiness.

Moritsuka had died empty.

"Well?" Shinoyama said. I stood up.

This didn't make sense. It didn't make sense at all.

This had never happened when I was at the FBI. Were my powers fading because I hadn't used them? Or…

"Th-the others," I wrapped my arms around my body and pleaded. "Go ask if there are others you've already ID'd that I can touch. Please."

"Okay." Shinoyama looked a little suspicious, but he went to talk to what appeared to be the man in charge.

I was given permission to touch several more bodies. A teenage girl. A young boy. A middle-aged corporate worker. A punkish-looking young man. A part-timer, a government worker. Their bodies, their possessions, their clothes. I used my powers on them all.

But all the movies I saw were the same as Moritsuka's. Everything was silent. Their hearts weren't moving at all.

There was nothing. They'd thrown themselves into the lake of their own will, silently and mechanically.

They had no reason to die at all. My powers hadn't faded.

Everyone's mind wavers a bit when faced with death, to a greater or lesser degree. A death chosen deliberately, even a peaceful one, was no exception. But...

It was like the 256 dead victims weren't even human.

Suddenly, my vision blurred and my knees buckled. I almost collapsed on top of a coffin.

"Are you okay?!" Shinoyama quickly grabbed me, which was the only reason I was able to stay upright.

"I'm sorry. I'm just a little tired."

"You've done enough for today."

"Yeah..." I brushed my bangs out of my eyes and realized my forehead was soaked with sweat. I'd been pushing myself harder than I'd thought. I'd never used my powers on a dozen bodies in a single day before.

Pain ran through my chest with each beat of my heart. It hurt a little to breathe. It was easy to imagine what would happen if I used my powers any more today.

But I still hadn't learned anything...

Bzzz...bzzzztttt...bzzz...

I heard an unfamiliar static in the quiet hall.

I looked around. It felt surprisingly close.

There was something large in one of the plastic cases near me that held the deceased's possessions. I went over to it, trying to control the pain in my chest.

"Hey, Kizaki."

"Let me check just one more body," I said, as I took a look at the case.

A keychain with what looked like a house key. A package of Kit-Kats. And...

A machine far larger than a dictionary.

What was it? I didn't know much about machines, so I couldn't tell what it did. Whatever it was, though, it was covered in switches.

"What is this?"

"It's an old radio," Shinoyama said. I stood up. "You don't see them around much anymore. It's the kind they used to sell when I was a kid. If it's here, it means it fell in the lake with the body. The water would have destroyed it."

The radio was in a plastic bag. I lifted it up. It was heavy. It probably wasn't because it was waterlogged; it was just this weight to begin with. The radio itself was inside a case with a shoulder strap so it could be carried easily. A doll from some anime was wrapped around the strap.

It was an old radio, but anything electronic like this was likely to leave good records. Maybe I could learn something from it that would help.

"May I borrow this for just twenty-four hours?"

"Do you need to?"

"I want to take a closer look at it." Ideally, I would touch it right away, but I'd used my psychometry too much today. My health probably wasn't going to allow that. Tomorrow, though...

Shinoyama sighed and nodded. "I'll come up with something to tell the chief. Bring it back in mint condition."

"Thank you." I was surprised that Shinoyama allowed me

to do anything that would mean extra work for him. Maybe my psychometry demonstration yesterday had paid off.

I moved my gaze back to the body in the coffin. It had already been ID'd. "Yuta Gamon," read the nametag on the plastic case next to the body. From the look of the body, he wasn't that much older or younger than me.

Why was he carrying this radio, then? Was he just really into radios or something?

I put my hand into the coffin and touched his cold forehead.

Begin the performance.

What I saw was…

Nothing.

…Nothing.

…Nothing.

Nothing at all.

Performance complete.

"What?!"

What was that? I hadn't seen a thing! No images. No sound. No voices. Nothing. This had never happened before.

Why? What was this boy?

And then…

"Th-that's me…"

I heard a voice in front of me. I looked up, and standing there, was…

"Huh?"

A boy who looked just like the one I'd just touched.

PARANORMAL SCIENCE NVL

Occultic;Nine

オカルティック・ナイン

THERE IS NO SUCH THING AS THE "OCCULT." IT CAN ALL BE DISPROVED BY SCIENCE.
ONLY THOSE WHO HAVE ACCEPTED EVERYTHING
HAVE THE RIGHT TO KNOW THE TRUTH.

▶ site 66: Yuta Gamon

"So I guess I'm just dancing to Zonko's tune. I'm not an 'I danced it' video dancer, I'm the admin of an aggregator blog now."

Yesterday, Zonko had suddenly started talking on a whim and had told me where the bodies were being kept. I stayed up all night, uncertain of what to do. By afternoon, I finally made the decision to head to Daiseiji.

As I got near the temple, I saw more and more people. A lot of parked cars, too. Normally, this was just a residential area, but now there were cars parked up against all the gates to the yards. I could tell from the places listed on the license plates that they didn't belong to the locals. Some of them were from out of town. All the people out walking were heading for the same place. Everybody looked solemn, and they were all pointing their heads down.

I joined with the crowd and headed to the temple.

In front of the temple were a bunch of media and several guards. People who'd come to see if the bodies of their family members were here were confronted by merciless flash photography and requests for interviews. I didn't see any gawkers. Probably nobody wanted to come to a place like this.

"It's going to be pretty hard to get in here…" What was I supposed to do if someone from the media shoved a microphone in my face? Even if I said "no comment," they'd still probably follow me around everywhere, and I certainly couldn't tell them I'd come to see my own body.

Maybe I should just go home.

I was scared now, so I turned to go.

"Where are you going?"

I heard a static-filled voice from the Skysensor again. She really only talked when it helped her, didn't she?

"Um, well, you know?"

"I know what?"

"Um…"

"So if you run here, what will you do next? Keep clinging to the impossible wish that you're not really dead?"

"If I tell Sarai or Toko about this place—"

"What, you'll ask them to see if your body's here? But even if they tell you it is, you're probably not going to believe them, are you? It's really important to see things with your own eyes. It shoves reality in your face so you can't deny it."

"You're talking like you're certain my body is here."

"Go see for yourself if it's certain or not! Jeez, you're such a pain!"

"It's not easy to admit that you're dead, okay?" I realized I was talking louder than I wanted to and quickly put my hand over my mouth. Even if there were a lot of media here, the area around us was quiet. If I talked loudly, it would echo pretty far.

Calm down. Don't let Zonko manipulate you anymore.

"Just go inside, okay?" she said.

"I don't want the media to see me."

"Nobody's going to be noticing you now. You're dead, after all. Hahaha!"

That's not funny.

Was Zonko doing this deliberately, knowing it would piss me off? But just like Zonko said, if I went home now, there would have been no point in coming. Plus if I went inside, it would give me a good story for Kirikiri Basara.

Screw whether it was appropriate or not. Hit counts were all that mattered.

"F-fine… I'll do it!" I charged into the row of cameras.

Daiseiji had a big gate, but it was closed right now, and the only way in was the service entrance right next to it. That's what everyone was using. Maybe it was to keep out the media. There were several guards at the gate who were questioning people who went in. It looked like the media weren't being allowed to pass.

I got right behind an old couple and pretended to be part of their family. Nobody questioned me as I went through the entrance. Evidently, they weren't checking people very thoroughly to keep the media and pranksters out. Or maybe they couldn't see me at all.

The temple hall was right past the entrance. I saw gloomy-looking people go in and out. Nobody was wearing funeral clothes, but it sure felt like a funeral. Just breathing the air made me want to throw up.

At the back of a hall was an eerie, black Buddha statue. The statue looked down silently on rows and rows of coffins.

There were so many white wooden coffins… all their lids were open so that the bodies inside could be seen. They were real bodies.

Although, compared to the bodies of Dr. Hashigami, or Myu-Pom's friend Chi, they were in much better condition, so it wasn't scary at all.

If my body was here, was it still in one piece, too? That made me feel just a little better. I didn't want to see myself with my face all messed up, or my limbs ripped off, or maybe my whole body unrecognizable to begin with.

"No, no… there's no way… there's no way I'm…here…" I wanted to run away, but my legs were drawn forward as if something was pulling me closer.

Suddenly, I saw a tiny girl stuffing her hand into one of the coffins in front of me. She was my age. She looked so pale that I almost imagined that she was one of the corpses who had gotten up and was walking around. Was she part of one of the families?

Right behind her was a gruff-looking older man who was watching over her with a worried expression. I took a closer look and saw there was a big plastic bag on top of the coffin. I recognized what was inside.

The Skysensor!

For a second I thought my heart had turned to ice. I quickly looked down at my chest. I was carrying the Skysensor, like I always did. It was slung over my shoulder in its usual place. That meant that whoever's Skysensor that was, it belonged to somebody else. Not many people had a retro radio like that these days, but the number probably wasn't zero.

That's right. It wasn't zero. That wasn't mine. Then I realized…

There was a Zonko tied to the Skysensor's strap.

"H-how…"

This was impossible.

Impossible.

Run. You can't stay here.

Don't look at anything else.

That's what my instincts were warning me to do, but I couldn't. My eyes turned on their own to the inside of the coffin the girl was sticking her hand into.

I shouldn't have looked. It didn't feel real at all. Even so, I froze in horror at the undeniable truth in front of me.

Inside the coffin…was my own body, pale like the color of clay.

"Th-that's me…" I said, and the girl looked up at me suddenly.

Our eyes met.

Did she hear my voice?

"You…?" The girl tried to talk to me, and then passed out and fell to the ground like a limp doll.

"H-hey! What's wrong? Kizaki!" the scary guy behind her shouted in surprise. He called over the police officers and had her taken to another room.

But I wasn't interested in that girl at all. I looked back at the body's face.

It was me. There was no mistaking it. I was dead, after all.

There was no denying it now. No making excuses. I'd found my own body.

This wasn't a dream.

Something caught in the back of my throat, and I couldn't breathe.

"Ah… aaah…" Dead.

I was dead.

"Aaah…" I cradled my head in my hands.

Somebody, please tell me it isn't true.

Tell me this is all some elaborate candid-camera thing.

Tell me the body is just some intricate thing made of wax.

"Aaaah—"

"Gamon!"

I gasped as somebody shook me by the shoulders. Toko and Sarai were next to me.

"Gamon… You saw it, huh?" Toko rubbed my upper arm gently. Her face was solemn.

Sarai was much quieter than usual, too. "Both Miss Sumikaze and I found our own as well."

That one sentence told me everything I needed to know.

They were here. In this place.

Sarai's body. Toko's body.

"Miyuu's coffin is here as well."

Even Myu-Pom…

I felt the strength draining from my body.

There was another coffin just behind me that I only barely managed to avoid slamming into. I recognized the body in it, too. I gasped as I looked at the nametag.

Shun Moritsuka.

That cosplaying jerk detective. That explained it. It had been after the 256 Incident when I talked to him.

"Ha…hahaha…."

I'd come here because Zonko had told me to, but I didn't think she was really telling the truth. Until I'd seen my own body, I'd held out some tiny shred of hope. I told myself there was no way I was really dead. There was no way my body was here. It was all just some big mistake.

"Th-this is all a lie. It's a dream." Even if my heart had given up, I was still speaking words of denial. "Come on, Sarai, this has to be a dream, right? It's not real, right? This isn't even 'occult' anymore!"

Sarai didn't answer. He was looking down at his feet, exhausted.

Come on, stop. Sarai, don't make that face.

"Come on, use your logic like you always do! It doesn't even matter if you're right or not! Come on, just rip this apart! Please, Sarai!"

Neither Sarai nor Toko said a word, and none of the other bodies—none of the other people—reacted to my scream.

PARANORMAL SCIENCE NVL

Occultic;Nine

オカルティック・ナイン

THERE IS NO SUCH THING AS THE "OCCULT." IT CAN ALL BE DISPROVED BY SCIENCE.

ONLY THOSE WHO HAVE ACCEPTED EVERYTHING

HAVE THE RIGHT TO KNOW THE TRUTH.

The first things I saw when I opened my eyes were the ceiling and the lights.

It was a medium-sized room with a tatami floor, and I was resting on top of a futon. There was nobody else in the room, but past the sliding doors I could hear people talking.

I looked at the clock. I'd been passed out for about a half hour. In a sense, it was only natural. I'd used my psychometry many times in a short period. I'd pushed myself too hard.

I bit my lip, got up, and looked at my face in the mirror on the wall. I looked awful. I looked more like a corpse than the bodies in the coffins. Still, I couldn't stay in here resting forever. I quickly brushed my messed-up hair and left the room.

"Kizaki. You're awake?" Shinoyama was in the smoking area outside, having a cigarette. The "smoking area" was just an ashtray in the corner of the parking lot. It was so smoky I didn't want to go anywhere near it, but the other detectives had told me it was Shinoyama who had carried me after I'd fallen unconscious, so I'd come to look for him.

"I'm sorry for the trouble. I'm okay now."

"Anemia?"

"Something like that." I nodded vaguely. "More importantly, about the last body I did psychometry on… There was a boy there who looked just like the body, right?"

"What did you say?" Shinoyama looked shocked.

"A boy about my age in a duffel coat."

"No, I don't think there was anybody like that."

"No, he was there. Just before I passed out."

Shinoyama thought for a second, and then shook his head. "I didn't see him. If he were there, I would've noticed."

Impossible…

I left the smoking area and went back into the temple. There were several police officers there, helping the families. I asked the same thing I'd asked Shinoyama, but the answer was always the same.

"Nobody but me saw that boy?"

That was impossible. There was no way. I'd seen him so clearly. I'd even heard his voice. I knew the difference between real memories and the ones I'd seen with my psychometry.

That boy was no hallucination.

The House of Crimson was as silent as ever today. It was so silent, my ears were starting to hurt.

I never played any music here. The only background noise was the sounds of the street from Harmonica Alley.

As I drifted between the faint noise and the silence, I worked on a new familiar doll, using a needle soaked for a week in the blood of a snake to stitch together the pieces of fabric to make the familiar's body. I hadn't even finished the face yet, but the design was already inside my head.

It felt like I hadn't seen any customers for days. I say "felt" because my memories were getting a little hazy.

How long had it been since I'd had a customer, if I didn't count that unpleasant detective from the other day? How long…?

Maybe it didn't matter. With my body gone, I didn't need to earn my daily bread or rest to recover from exhaustion. Even so, just like I'd done in life, I left for the store in the morning and spent my day alone in the emptiness.

Even without my body, my mind remained here in the mortal world. That seemed like it meant I was supposed to suffer the way I always did.

My eyes started to feel numb, perhaps because I'd been working in the gloomy room. I sighed a bit and put down the needle, then rubbed my temples with my thumbs before opening up my tablet to check the time. I'd been very curious about the time for a while now, but the more I thought about it, the slower time seemed to go.

My nerves were so tired. So much had happened lately that I was mentally exhausted. Today it was exhaustion from nervousness.

That's enough work for today. I moved the partially completed familiar to the shelf behind me and looked ahead.

I saw the dusty interior of the room and the entrance to the shop, and next to the door…

"Welcome," I said, and there was an answer.

Yeah.

It was the voice of the devil, but there was something different today.

"I had always imagined you in a more terrible form."

I was looking at a man in black, floating in the air with his legs crossed. He was far older than me, it seemed. He was probably in his twenties. He wore a black coat and black boots, and sharp-looking eyes poked out from the gaps in his long black hair.

I looked directly back into those eyes. Just staring. To tell him that I saw him, too.

He seemed to notice. *I figured you could see me.*

"You're…the devil, aren't you?" My voice felt like it was going to start shaking. Tension, fear, uncertainty, and…a certain sense of excitement that the devil had revealed himself.

I was face-to-face with the devil right now. When I'd seen the devil in the form of a man walking right through the door like it wasn't even there, I'd almost screamed. I'd known the man wasn't human, and the one being I knew who wasn't human was the devil.

We'd known each other for over two years, but this was my first time actually seeing him. Why was he just staring at me? Why wasn't he saying anything? I didn't know why he was doing this, and that was so eerie that I was frozen in fear and couldn't even stand up. His gaze was so terrifying, I hadn't been able to concentrate on my work.

"Have you always been watching me like that?"

I don't have that kind of time. I ain't yer guardian angel. He told me I was wrong in a sharp tone.

I let out a sigh of relief that I'd gotten the answer I expected.

What was a little surprising was that the devil in front of me was very tall, with a handsome face—and he looked like a completely normal human.

Even if he didn't look like a monster, I'd still expected at least black wings on his back, since he was a devil, but there wasn't anything like that. Of course, he did have a murderous aura about him, like touching him would rip my hand apart as if it had been cut to shreds by a knife. That was certainly demonic.

"Why have you shown yourself to me today?"

The devil didn't answer at first. He just stared at me coldly, not even uncrossing his legs. I couldn't bear his gaze, so I tried to say something else, but he cut me off.

It ain't me. You're the one who changed.

"Me?" I hadn't even considered that, but once the devil pointed it out, it made the most sense. "I see. I already have more than one foot in the grave. That's what you mean, right?"

Who knows?

"Then I haven't come any closer to you?"

You and I are different. And if you think anybody can be a devil, you're wrong.

The devil always refused to give me clear answers. He would always push me away, but that was fine. That was what made him my devil.

"Earlier I said I could hear your voice clearly now, remember? At that point, it seems I was already dead."

You wanted to die, right?

"Huh?"

Well? How does it feel to be dead?

That question was slightly unexpected. "I-I'm not sure how to answer that. It doesn't feel real." I tilted my head with uncertainty. "But since I'm dead, I'd like to see my brother."

The devil uncrossed his legs and went to slip through the door again.

"U-um… wait…" I called for him to stop. I'd never done this before. The old me would never try to get the devil to stay.

Don't start trying to boss me around.

As I expected, the devil pushed me away. I swallowed my words, uncertain of why I'd done that.

Why did I tell him to stop? Was it because I could see him now? Or perhaps…

You don't really believe in devils, do you?

The curse that detective had put on me had been echoing in my mind. It ate away at my will and tried to control me.

Don't get any ideas about following me, the devil said. *We're not friends. We're business partners. You know that, right, girl?*

"Yes…" My head drooped. By looking down, I hoped to break my obsession with him.

A whim of the devil's. It was up to him if he came or not. That had always been the rule. So we should always obey that rule.

I looked up after a while and the devil was already gone. I stared at the closed door that he'd probably left by.

The words left my mouth unconsciously. "Who…are you?"

They echoed throughout the tiny shop before being erased by the silence.

PARANORMAL SCIENCE NVL

Occultic;Nine

オカルティック・ナイン

THERE IS NO SUCH THING AS THE "OCCULT." IT CAN ALL BE DISPROVED BY SCIENCE.
ONLY THOSE WHO HAVE ACCEPTED EVERYTHING
HAVE THE RIGHT TO KNOW THE TRUTH.

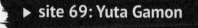

▶ site 69: Yuta Gamon

Even after locking myself up in my house like a real NEET god, I didn't feel any better.

I hadn't been able to sleep last night. At some point, morning had come. My body heavy, I forced myself out of bed and looked out the window.

"It's true... I'm really dead..." I whispered the words aloud, and the despair came pouring in and ruined my morning.

The air felt heavy. Heavy, and cold.

I thought once you were dead, you just stopped feeling anything. Personally, I would have preferred that. Then I wouldn't have to suffer and be so miserable.

I looked towards the desk. My laptop was on it and still turned on. The monitor displayed Kirikiri Basara's web page.

It was the article I'd uploaded before about the 256 Incident. Since I hadn't known I was one of the 256, I'd written it in my usual joking style.

The comments were the same as ever. The Basariters were,

like always, gathering at the site and making rude comments. It was true even after so much time had passed since the incident.

[Urban Legend] Anybody Care About the 256 Incident?

This morning, the Mitaka Police Department announced to the media that they'd discovered a massive amount of drowned bodies in the lake. 256 bodies were discovered.

The cause of death in each case was drowning, and the most prominent theory is that they all dove in of their own accord.

The Scientific Investigation Laboratory has yet to say whether any kind of drugs were discovered in the bodies, and it is hoped that further announcements will be forthcoming.

■NEET God

> 256 lol
> Did a computer do it? And is that lake even big enough to fit 256 people lol
> So I've got three theories right now.

① Cult Mass Hypnosis

② Some internet suicide site asked for volunteers for a big meeting.

③ A bunch of people decided to have a swimming party in Inokashira and it turned out the water was poison and they all died lol

④ After an alien abduction the aliens threw all the bodies in the lake lol

⑤ HAARP mind control

⑥ A Tengu did it

Something like that lol
Alright Basariters, slice this shit to ribbons

369: Anonymous Streaming Live

You see the victim list?
Is Miyuu Aikawa Myu-tan?

371: Anonymous Streaming Live

Myu... that's a shock.

372: Anonymous Streaming Live

Saw it
I guess it's true...

373: Anonymous Streaming Live

Why?
She just told my fortune!

375: Anonymous Streaming Live

No way...

376: Anonymous Streaming Live

Nononono
Its a lie its a lie its a lie

378: Anonymous Streaming Live

Depressing

379: Anonymous Streaming Live

Was she mental?

386: Anonymous Streaming Live

I heard a friend of hers was murdered

So maybe she killed herself then

387: Anonymous Streaming Live

Maybe something was bothering her

That was a group suicide, right?

391: Anonymous Streaming Live

>>386

Is that true

Where'd you read that?

394: Anonymous Streaming Live

>>386

Fake news dude

396: Anonymous Streaming Live

Maybe she broke up with a boyfriend?

397: Anonymous Streaming Live

Killed herself from the shock?

And took the other 255 with her?

400: Anonymous Streaming Live

She's not a psychic or anything lol

401: Anonymous Streaming Live

That happened with some weird religion a long time ago, right?

They formed a colony with their leader and everyone drank the

Kool-Aid.

403: Anonymous Streaming Live
>>401
Did they go to space?

404: Anonymous Streaming Live
Colony like a village, dumbass.

405: Anonymous Streaming Live
I can't believe it...

406: Anonymous Streaming Live
Suicide is wrong!

407: Anonymous Streaming Live
So what was the cause exactly?

408: Anonymous Streaming Live
She wasn't well mentally.
I remember that time a listener made her cry.

409: Anonymous Streaming Live
What? Seriously?
What? What happened?

410: Anonymous Streaming Live
Man, occult streamers are all fucking batshit crazy, aren't they?

411: Anonymous Streaming Live
I wondered why KiriBasa was so active... I guess this is why...

412: Anonymous Streaming Live
That encounter with SARAI must've really shook her.

414: Anonymous Streaming Live
| Why...

415: Anonymous Streaming Live
| Seriously? I can't stop shaking.

416: Anonymous Streaming Live
| SARAI get your ass out here.
| Kill yourself fucker

417: Anonymous Streaming Live
| What did SARAI do?

418: Anonymous Streaming Live
| Shut down Myu's live stream.

419: Anonymous Streaming Live
| There was somebody with a similar name to SARAI on the list,
| wasn't there?
| Dunno if it's the same guy.
| http://www.foreistage.jp/news/4+331182045/

420: Anonymous Streaming Live
| Huh? Really?

421: Anonymous Streaming Live
| >>419
| SARAI's dead too

422: Anonymous Streaming Live
| So it's like a curse?

423: Anonymous Streaming Live
| They got him too, huh?

424: Anonymous Streaming Live
| I wonder if they were wearing clothes when they were found.

425: Anonymous Streaming Live
| What were you imagining lol

Most of the comments were about Myu-Pom, and there wasn't any info on the 256 Incident.

It was weird how excited the Basariters were. Because I was part of this—and because I knew Myu-Pom and Sarai, too—I didn't feel like celebrating in the slightest.

"These guys are crazy." Maybe I shouldn't say this, since I was the one who put together the article, but looking at the comments, I felt more scared than angry. They were attacking, egging on, and insulting… that's all they did. Nobody was showing any sympathy, or pity, or telling people when they'd gone too far to cut it out.

If anybody did, they'd just be treated like a troll and ganged up on until they stopped ruining everybody's fun. So no matter what awful things somebody said, they would just be ignored. People would just go with whatever the most popular opinion was. Or maybe they'd just find one guy who got a little too excited and try to troll him.

None of them seemed to feel like they had any responsibility for this. It was easier that way; nobody had to get hurt.

"Sarai was really important, huh?" Looking objectively at the mess that was going on online, I realized once more how important he was.

Even if people attacked or made fun of him, Sarai was never thrown off. He just kept on promoting his own theories. Of course, he had no backup at all. Even in the face of concentrated firepower, he never changed his style.

I could never do that. No matter what situation I was in, I didn't want to be attacked. I wanted to be liked. I wanted to be praised. I just wanted them to say things that made me feel good. If I felt I was alone, that would be enough to make me feel scared.

"Mom..." I slowly left the room.

There was nobody in the living room. I hadn't slept at all, so of course I'd noticed that my mom hadn't come home.

Come to think of it... how had Mom reacted when Dad died? I'd been so busy thinking about my own sadness that I'd never thought about how she was feeling.

It was just after Dad had died, but Mom had spent her time making sure the funeral went off without a hitch, even going around to thank everyone who'd attended. I could only remember seeing her from behind. I couldn't remember what kind of face she'd made.

"Was it Mom who ID'd my body after they pulled it up from the lake, I wonder?"

Sarai had said they'd waited to announce names until the bodies and their possessions had been ID'd by friends or relatives. In my case, my mom was my only relative.

My mom was strong. She made enough money to go out and have fun while still providing for her loser of a son. My mom was a hardworking career woman, and I respected her almost as much as I respected Dad.

What had her face looked like when she'd seen my body? I couldn't imagine it. Was she acting strong, like she had with Dad, and getting the funeral ready in-between working her job?

I looked at the clock. It was still 10:00 AM.

Maybe she'd been up all night working? Sure, she could be a bit of a workaholic, but she'd never just not come home before. Had she been involved in some kind of accident?

"Oh…"

Suddenly, my eyes settled on the paper on the dinner table— and then I realized what it was I couldn't speak.

How long had it been there?

How had I not seen it?

It was a single, ordinary-looking piece of paper that was a little bit crumpled. Had she copied it somewhere, or gotten it from the police?

It was a list of names. The paper was covered with them, 256 in all from top to bottom. A single name was underlined with red pen.

"Yuta Gamon."

"Oh… that's it."

It wasn't that Mom wasn't coming home. She…couldn't come home.

I let out a sob.

I'm an idiot. The biggest idiot in the world. How come I hadn't noticed something so obvious?

The tears came pouring down as I cried loudly. "What am I… what the hell am I?"

Dad died, and I got depressed and locked myself in my room. Even now, with all that was going on, I was still making my mother sad. I was just sobbing and getting depressed and locking myself in my room. I was pathetic. I really was the worst. I couldn't even do anything for the mom I'd left behind.

I couldn't do anything... I'd just float here like a ghost... I couldn't do anything!

▶ site 70: Asuna Kizaki

The first thing I did when I woke up in the morning was visit the Musashino Police Station. I wanted to get the documents I'd asked Shinoyama for.

One of them was a list of the victims from the Inokashira Mass Suicide. About two hundred of them had been identified so far. The other was the location of FM-KCZ, the hint I'd gotten from Moritsuka.

I left the station and headed into the Dotour's in front of Mitaka Station. It was still morning, so the coffee shop was still empty. I sat in one of the seats in the corner. The soy milk latte was delicious, with just the perfect amount of sweetness, and it made me feel a little better.

When I was in America, I'd liked sweet drinks, but ever since I'd come to Japan my tastes had changed. I thought about that as I paged through the list of suicide victims. I was looking for a specific name.

"There it is."

Yuta Gamon.

His was the body where I'd "not seen anything" when I used my psychometry at Daiseiji yesterday. Surprisingly, he was a second-year student at Seimei High. In other words, he went to my school.

He lived in Kichijoji. No siblings. Only living relative, a mother. His dad had died seven years ago. There was nothing particularly eye-catching in his profile.

Why hadn't I seen anything? I looked through the other names on the list and quickly found Moritsuka's name.

I remembered what I'd seen when I replayed the body's memories, and my chest ached. Why did they—the 256, including Moritsuka—have to die?

Right now, everything about this case was a mystery. The more I investigated, the more the mysteries deepened. It was like a bottomless swamp. Even in my time at the FBI, I'd never encountered such a bizarre crime as this.

"I'll just have to follow the clue Moritsuka gave me, I guess." I took the other document out of its clear folder.

FM-KCZ, the mini-FM radio station. Next to its address was a memo with extra information. I'd told Shinoyama and Kozaki that I only needed the address, but they'd gone above and beyond what I'd asked for.

According to the memo, there was only one person in Kichijoji with a terrestrial broadcasting license who'd died in the last ten years. Private FM radio stations required a license if you wanted to broadcast over a wide area; otherwise you were violating the law.

And the name of that person was—

"Koresuke Gamon..."

Gamon...

I turned back to the list of suicide victims and checked Yuta Gamon's name. "It's the same."

Yuta Gamon's deceased father. His name was Koresuke Gamon. Which meant that Yuta Gamon was the son of the operator of FM-KCZ.

It was a strange coincidence. Or did it mean something?

I looked at the radio I had next to me. It was the one I'd borrowed from Yuta Gamon's body at Daiseiji yesterday. Maybe this had belonged to his father. It was big and heavy, maybe because it was old. Still, there were signs that it had been kept at his side at all times. A symbol of the bond between a child and his dead father, maybe?

Yesterday, my health had made reading it too risky to do, but now...

I took off my gloves and softly touched the radio.

Begin the performance.

I wanted to replay the thirty minutes leading up to its owner's death.

The image was displayed on the screen. I gasped when I saw it.

The image was clear, like a high-definition TV, and the view wasn't cramped at all. I'd touched countless objects and people to replay their memories, but I'd never seen something so clearly before.

It was Yuta Gamon's house. His room was messy, and his floor was covered with manga, but the radio was placed carefully on the table. That was where I was seeing this from.

There was a lump on the bed. Sometimes it moved, so Gamon

was probably asleep. Nothing happened for a while, but suddenly, after a bit, Yuta Gamon woke up.

He was completely silent. Everybody stretches and moans a little when they get up, but this time, Gamon didn't. He quickly changed from his pajamas into his clothes in smooth and fluid movements. Even though his hair was a mess, he did nothing to fix it.

The last thing he did was put on his duffel coat and then reach out to touch the radio. His face was…

Blank, like he was dreaming. His eyes weren't focused at all, but his steps and movements were strangely sure. Sleepwalking? The list hadn't gone into his medical history.

Gamon put the radio over his shoulder, then put on his shoes and headed out, even going so far as to lock the door. There was no hesitation in his steps as he took the shortest route to Inokashira Park.

He finally arrived there. Many people with the same vacant gaze as his had already gathered. What I would see now was probably the same thing I'd seen from Moritsuka and the other victims, but the amount of information I could get from this video was completely different. I carefully stared at the screen.

Gamon slowly walked into the water like the others, watching those in front of him sink without blinking, and when it was his turn, he glanced down at the water. The moon wavered on the water's surface. Gamon leaned back like he was about to jump, and then fell backwards into the water.

"I'm sorry."

What was that?!

Performance complete.

That was the only information I could get out of the radio. I looked up and I was back in Dotour's.

Whose voice had that been?

The voice had been carved into the radio's memories. It was the clear voice of a cute, young girl. It wasn't Gamon's.

Inokashira Park was silent except for the sound of the water. That's why the sudden female voice had left such a strong impression.

"Yuta Gamon is full of mysteries, huh?" Just then, a message came in on my phone. "Hello?"

"I've got information on the Hachifukushin," Oliver said, without even bothering to identify himself. This wasn't just some quirk of his. It was common in the FBI. "I'll send over what I've got." And then he hung up. That was ordinary, too.

"The Hachifukushin…" It was a weird name, come to think of it. The Shichifukushin, or Seven Gods of Blessing, were pretty common. Had they added one to them?

I opened the mail app on my phone and looked at the message I'd received.

"This is…!" I gasped when I saw it. "There's a connection here… did Moritsuka notice this?" I shivered as the puzzle pieces began to fall into place.

Occultic;Nine

PARANORMAL SCIENCE NVL

THERE IS NO SUCH THING AS THE "OCCULT." IT CAN ALL BE DISPROVED BY SCIENCE.
ONLY THOSE WHO HAVE ACCEPTED EVERYTHING
HAVE THE RIGHT TO KNOW THE TRUTH.

▶ site 71: Yuta Gamon

It had been seven years since my dad had died, but FM-KCZ was right where it had been.

It was five minutes from the condo where I lived—definitely past tense now—with my mom. It was a radio station, but on the outside, it looked like an ordinary house. This had been my dad's parents' house. He'd remodeled the first floor into a radio studio. The inside was far more elaborate than one would expect from the term "mini-FM radio station."

It had been seven years since I'd been here. In other words, I hadn't been here once since Dad died. Maybe it would be better to say I was avoiding it. I was deliberately avoiding coming anywhere near it.

So why had I come here now? Did I want to escape from this painful reality by remembering my kind father? Or was it because I thought Mom was here?

I approached the house. It was two stories tall, with a front door facing the street and a big window to the first-floor studio. Mom would come by sometimes to clean it, and it was clean enough that you'd never believe it was empty. The big antenna on the second-floor roof was still there, sticking out like a sore thumb in the quiet residential neighborhood.

I looked in through the window at the studio.

It was empty. Mom wasn't here, it seemed. I used to love watching my dad's excitement through the window as he did his recording.

During broadcasts I would always stand here, using the dial on the Skysensor to tune in and make sure I could hear my dad's voice. Then I'd look at him through the window and give him a thumbs-up.

He'd do the same, and the program would begin.

"Once again, we've started off with my son watching me. Welcome to Musashino Wonderland."

That was always how he'd start the program.

Whenever I watched him through that window, I was so proud, and excited, and happy. I always used to look forward to the days when my dad did his broadcasts.

I sighed and stood in front of the window as I flipped the switch on the Skysensor. I spun the dial without looking at the numbers, relying only on the sensation of my fingers.

Bzzztt...bzzzzt...

Static came out of the speaker. Just like I'd tried before.

No matter how long I waited, even after I was dead, would I never be able to connect with my dad?

"Yuta Gamon."

"Hyah!"

Suddenly, somebody said my name from behind me, and I thought my heart would stop even though I wasn't alive.

I turned around to see a girl who was my age, or a little younger than me. Our eyes met.

"Can I talk to you for a second?"

Huh? Hadn't I met her somewhere? Saeko Kitaya? No, that girl was much plainer. This girl was... I dunno, this is a weird example, but the word that came to mind was "colorless."

I didn't know anyone this colorless. Then who was she? No, forget that!

"You can see me? Can you see me? Hey, can you see me?!"

"Yes." The girl nodded. "I don't know why, honestly."

Zzzzz...bbbbzzz...

Huh? I was hearing the static from the radio again, but it wasn't from the one on my shoulder.

I looked and saw that the girl in front of me was carrying a bag, too. It looked incredibly like mine. No, it didn't "look like it." That bag for the Skysensor had been my own design, and there was even the same Zonko strap on it.

"That's...my Skysensor!"

"Sky- what?" The girl's eyebrows narrowed.

"Skysensor! That radio! A BCL radio made in 1975! It's the greatest masterpiece of that famous manufacturer! It's capable of capturing every radio wave across the planet! Wait, that doesn't matter!" I strode towards the girl and stared at the Zonko keychain. "This! Zonko! It's Zonko!"

The girl simply looked confused.

"Is a coincidence like this possible? No way! It can't be this identical! Were you copying me? Are you a stalker? A beautiful girl like you as a stalker... are you some kind of yandere?"

"I got this from your corpse."

"Well, it doesn't matter. It would take more than two identical radios to surprise me at this point. I'm already dead, after all."

"I'd like to talk to you about that." The girl didn't seem surprised at all to hear me say that I was dead. She was a very calm girl. She didn't feel like she was really my age. "I'm investigating the Inokashira Mass Suicide."

"Investigating? Wait, who are you?" I looked again at the girl in front of me. This time I tried my best to be subtle so our eyes wouldn't meet.

She had a kid's face and a tiny, fragile-looking body. She didn't look very healthy. Her skin was pale, and her pallor was pretty bad. She was clearly the sick-character archetype. She was thin enough that I thought she might be in middle school. At least, I was sure she wasn't in college.

She hadn't smiled at all, either. Was she the type who didn't let her emotions show? The so-called Ayanami type. In every way, she was the exact opposite of Ryotasu.

So what did she mean she was "investigating" the case?

Was she playing detective? All on her own? Or did she run an occult aggregator blog like I did? Maybe she'd decided I was a rival and was stalking me? I didn't need any stalkers, but maybe I could hire her as a third Basara girl?

As I stood there thinking about that, the girl in front of me said something I'd never expected. She took what looked like a black pass case out of her pocket, opened it, and showed it to me. "I'm Asuna

Kizaki. I'm an FBI investigator in charge of the Kichijoji incident."

"Huhuhh?!" I yelled in shock. "Seriously? FBI? Like *the* FBI?" I checked the ID she showed me. It was the same as I'd seen in movies and things, sure enough. It even had her photo. "Oh, wow! A Japanese FBI Agent who's also a hot girl? It's like something out of a manga!"

"U-um…"

"No, no, no. Hold on. This is impossible. The FBI's American police! They'd never come to Kichijoji. In other words, you're lying. Are you cosplaying or something? I don't think I remember that character. Were there any moe FBI characters in anime?"

"It's not cosplay. The FBI is interested in the case that's happening in this town right now. It's that important." She looked back at me seriously. Just looking at her, she didn't seem to be lying. But still…

"So the FBI just specially made you an officer? Just one day?"

"There was another officer in charge, but now I've taken over. Until a year ago, I was in America, where I worked for the FBI."

"That doesn't answer the question. There's no way the FBI would hire a young girl like you. You're my age, or younger than me, right?"

"I'm older than you. I'm a third-year student at Seimei High."

"See? So you're a Japanese high school hot girl FBI agent. Another improbable story. Nobody's going to believe that. Is this an anime? It's an anime, right? There's no way you're telling the truth!"

"I'm telling the truth!"

"Well, I guess it doesn't matter whether you are or not."

Since I was dead, she didn't have anything to do with me. If I just considered her a slightly delusional upperclassman, it wasn't that big a deal. After dealing with Ryotasu all the time, this was nothing.

For now, I would call this "Japanese high school hot girl FBI agent," a.k.a. Asuna Kizaki, "Asunyan." Just like with Myu-Pom, if I ended up writing any articles about her, it would make her more popular. Still, if I was going to meet an FBI agent, I would've preferred to meet Mulder and Scully. I couldn't speak English, though.

Using the key, I invited Asunyan into FM-KCZ. The inside of the station was a little dusty, but it smelled just like I remembered, and I almost teared up a little.

"So, um, what do you want with me?"

"Why did you kill yourself?" Asunyan asked. She evidently wasn't concerned with my feelings as a dead person.

"I did not kill myself. I'm dead, I guess, but it wasn't suicide."

"So you were killed?"

"I don't remember that at all. It took a while for me to even realize I was dead. Well, I guess that happens a lot with ghosts! Hahaha." I laughed, a little forced. Then I remembered what happened at Daiseiji yesterday and immediately felt depressed. "Yeah, I really saw my own body… it was awful. I should never have gone. Man, I should've never gone! Damn it!"

Hmm? Wait a second. Wasn't she…

"Oh, right! You were the girl next to my coffin yesterday!"

"That's right. We met yesterday at Daiseiji."

I see. That's why I remembered her.

"You don't look so good," I said.

"I'm fine now. Don't worry about me," Asunyan answered as she looked around the inside of the booth. Her expression was serious, and not at all like a girl playing detective. "This was your dad's radio station, right?"

"Yeah. It was a small one, but it had a decent number of listeners. We got a bunch of postcards and stuff, and I think we were pretty famous, I guess."

There was a cork bulletin board on the wall of the booth, covered with letters and postcards my dad had received. There was a good number of thank-you letters. After seven years, they were pretty faded, but they were still legible. Most of the letters were about things that didn't matter, but those that did, Dad would read on air and try his best to help them with any problems they were having.

Thinking back, for what was only a tiny radio station you could hear in Kichijoji, he got a lot of letters like that.

"Your father's name was…Koresuke Gamon."

"Right! You know my dad? I never thought he'd have any listeners in the FBI! Was he super popular in America or something?" I asked jokingly, but Asunyan didn't laugh at all. Her face was calm and collected.

How'd she know my dad's name? Was she really a stalker, maybe?

"I'm here investigating the Inokashira Mass Suicide—"

"The 256 Incident."

"Two-five-six? What?"

"That's the name I came up with. Oh, the FBI can use it. I won't ask for royalties."

"The 256 Incident…right. In the process of working on the case, this station's name came up."

"What kind of connection is there between my dad and the 256 Incident?"

"I discovered that your father was involved with a certain group."

"Huh?" A certain group?

"The Hachifukushin Circle. Have you ever heard of it?"

I shook my head. "What's that?"

"A kind of spiritual seminar, as they're sometimes called. Your father was very popular there."

"Spiritual… what?" I wasn't sure what I was hearing. "Listen, don't talk about my dad that way. He was just a normal guy who started up an FM radio station for fun—"

"As he answered letters with people's problems on-air, many people came to rely on Koresuke Gamon. Eventually, he started holding seminars where he could speak to them directly." Asunyan was staring right at me. Her way of speaking had changed a little. It was…strange. There wasn't any harshness to her tone, but it felt like it was putting me on my guard. "In the end, it became a religious corporation."

"A religious corporation?!"

I hadn't heard that at all. Not a thing about it. Dad had never talked about it, and neither had Mom.

"The Hachifukushin Circle was a religious corporation intended to help those in need. At first, it functioned as a sort of hospice. They took in people who hospitals said they couldn't help, or those who disliked or didn't trust doctors. But eventually it became a kind of cult."

A cult. I snapped when I heard that negative word. "I don't know anything about that!" I stood up from my chair and stalked towards Asunyan. "My dad was the leader of some kind of cult? No way! Don't talk about my dad like that!"

"That's not what I'm here to do." Asunyan looked a little bothered, but she didn't flinch or turn away. "But the Hachifukushin Circle and FM-KCZ are both probably related to what you call the 256 Incident!"

"Shut up! You're not even really with the FBI! You're just making things up! Don't try to intrude into my private life with your fantasies!"

"They aren't fantasies, and I'm not making stuff up!" Now it was her turn to get emotional. "Those were the last hints he left me before he died!" she yelled.

The two of us glared at each other, only a few centimeters apart. But it was Asunyan who looked away first.

"I'm sorry." She took an awkward step away from me.

"Wh-what? I'm talking to you because you wanted to talk. Why are you trying to make things worse for me when I'm already dead?"

"That wasn't what I wanted to do…"

Wait, who was "he," anyway?

"I can't be at the center of all this… it's a coincidence. I'm not the hero of a light novel or anything. The whole 'the hero is actually dead' trope got played out a long time—"

"I'm sorry for talking about this without thinking about how you'd feel. But I'm not lying. I have proof. Look at this." Asunyan took a phone out of her pocket. "This digital data contains the magazines put out by the Hachifukushin Circle."

I looked down, afraid, at the smartphone.

There was a group photo with many people in it. It was a picture of an empty-looking room, like you might see at a hospital, but there were more than two dozen people in it, of all different ages and sexes. At the center of all of them, smiling, was…

"Dad…" So was Asunyan telling the truth, then? Just looking at this photo couldn't tell me if it was a cult or not.

It did, however, prove my dad was involved with the Hachifukushin Circle, and that he'd died without telling me.

"Why didn't Dad tell me anything before he died? Was it because I was just a kid?"

"Or maybe there was a reason he couldn't," Asuna said.

"What reason is good enough to not tell your own family?"

Asunyan didn't answer, but that's how I knew exactly what she was trying to say.

"Are you trying to tell me Dad was up to something bad?"

Asunyan had just called it a cult. A cult religion. This was a side of my father I knew nothing about.

"A-anyway, this is all just a lie. What are you hoping to get out of lying to me?"

"Right now, I want every clue I can get my hands on, and it seems to me like you're deeply involved in this. So help me." Her expression was pleading. She looked desperate. She didn't look like a detective who was researching a case because it was her job. It felt like she had some other kind of attachment to it.

"I'm deeply involved in the case, huh? Is that what they call 'detective's intuition'?"

Asunyan chuckled. "I don't think I have that, but…"

She took off the glove on her right hand and touched the microphone in the DJ booth.

Asunyan closed her eyes slowly. What was she going to do? It felt somehow like I shouldn't approach her or say anything. I gulped.

It only lasted a few seconds, and then she exhaled softly and opened her eyes. Then she started to talk.

"The postcards are in the right side of the drawer. It was your job to put the letters and postcards in there. The name of the program was Musashino Wonderland. You would always wait outside the booth with that radio, the Skysensor, and then your dad wouldn't start broadcasting until you had turned it on. You'd give up him a thumbs-up as a signal. He always started the program the same way. 'Once again, we've started off with my son watching me. Welcome to Musashino Wonderland.'"

It was like she was reading my memories. Everything she said was just how I remembered it.

"H-how…do you know about my dad?"

Asunyan put her glove back on and shrugged a little. "I don't have a detective's intuition, but I do have stuff that's a little bit different. That's how I'm an FBI agent at this age."

Did she have special powers? This was even more like a manga.

"Are you a psychometer?"

"Huh? Y-yes. You know about us, huh?" Asunyan was shocked that I'd guessed her power.

"There's a lot of them in manga."

"I-I've never had anyone tell me that before." Maybe it wasn't that popular a superpower in America.

"Oh wow. A superpowered high school girl FBI agent, huh? You've got all kinds of stuff going on." That would explain how she got to be an FBI agent at her age. "So it wasn't cosplay, then."

"I guess you believe me." She turned back towards me, relieved. "I'll tell you everything I find out about your dad, so…please help me."

I knew she wasn't a bad person, and that there were things about Dad I didn't know. I was curious, but I didn't want to get myself involved too much.

So what could I ask for in exchange?

"I'm willing to help, but then let me report on this."

"Report?"

"I run a blog called Kirikiri Basara." I pulled out my phone and showed her the web page. "Can you let me do a special on you, as a 'Japanese High School Hot Girl FBI Psychometer'? I was already planning on doing a special on Myu-Pom, the 'Cute Popular High School Girl Fortune-Teller.' A lot's happened, and I haven't done it yet. I'm sure if I did a special on that, I'd get tons of hits on my website. If you're okay with that, then I'm willing to help."

If I was dead, the least I could do was try and get some hits for my blog. At this point, I practically didn't even care.

"Your blog… okay. But keep me anonymous, all right?"

"You can leave that to me. I'm planning on introducing you as Asunyan."

"Huh?" Asunyan blinked at me in surprise.

"It's a nickname. You can call me by my nickname, too. Or maybe just call me 'Yuta'!"

"Wait." Asunyan cut me off. "Let me check something. I did tell you that I was from Seimei, right? And that I already graduated?"

"Oh, so maybe I should call you 'Miss Asunyan'?"

"That's not the issue. I'm older than you, you know that, right?"

"Wow, are you the type that thinks about stuff like that? Like a musclebrain type? You don't seem that way at all. I'm really surprised."

Asunyan sighed, then looked down and started to whisper. "Avoids confronting people head-on. Instead, chooses to joke and change the subject. Has probably run from confronting things for years…"

Wait, was that my profile? Wow, I guess she really was an FBI agent. She was pretty accurate, too. Well, I mean, I knew it. I was a scummy ghost affiliate-blog admin, after all.

"So anyway, Asunyan, I want you to wear cat ears during the interview. Or maybe a jacket with a cat-ear hood, like Myu-Pom."

"If you call me Asunyan one more time, I'll rip off every fastener on that duffel coat of yours, starting from the top."

"S-scary! You really are a musclebrain!"

That kind of gap wasn't something we needed. These days, being violent not only wasn't a positive trait for a heroine, but it was also enough to make people hate you.

Paranormal Science NVL

Occultic;Nine

オカルティック・ナイン

There is no such thing as the "Occult." It can all be disproved by science.
Only those who have accepted everything
have the right to know the truth.

▶ site 72: Asuna Kizaki

When I was in the FBI, I was on the special investigations team, where I used my superpower called psychometry. Yet, even though I had a special power, I never believed in ghosts.

Sure, even in America people talked about the occult. Actually, they believed in it more than we did. But all the criminals I ever dealt with were living people. Even the strangest cases always came down to tricks or natural phenomena. Maybe that's why, ever since I was a little girl, I never believed in the occult.

Come to think of it, Moritsuka always talked to me about the occult with that innocent smile of his. No matter how many times I told him it wasn't real, he always said the same thing.

"But don't you think it would be more interesting if it did exist?"

Right in front of me there was a ghost—if you could call him that.

It really did exist.

The ghost was right here with me in the booth at a small,

abandoned radio station. Everything I'd discussed with Yuta Gamon made my head hurt. Maybe this was all a dream. If it was, I hoped I could wake up.

I glanced down at the radio—Gamon had just told me it was called a Skysensor—that I was holding. Maybe it was because I was holding this that I could see him. I used my psychometry by mentally flipping a switch, but there was a chance that my power was still leaking out.

Did that mean if I carried something of Moritsuka's, I'd be able to see him, too? No, that was stupid. It was avoiding reality. I drove the scene, which was rapidly starting to resemble a romance movie, out of my mind.

"Listen, um, Asunya—I mean, Kizaki. There's one more thing I'd like your help with."

"One more thing?" I tensed up a little, expecting him to ask for money. But the next words he spoke were serious.

"Can you catch the person who killed Myu-Pom's friend?"

"Myu-Pom? Who's that?"

"Oh, her real name is Miyuu Aikawa. She's Basara Girl Number Two. She does fortune-telling via livestream. She was the fortune-teller I just mentioned…and one of the 256."

Fortune-telling, huh? That sort of uncertain stuff had never been a part of my life, so I didn't really understand it.

"Myu-Pom's friend was just killed. And they haven't caught the person who did it."

"When was 'just'? Where?"

"A place called Enmeiji."

I instantly remembered. Shinoyama had told me about

that case, where the victim was a student at Seimei, just like me and Gamon.

"I see. So you knew the victim."

"Indirectly." He was a little weird, but he seemed to really care. Maybe I'd had the wrong idea about Gamon—a little.

"I'm with the FBI, so I can't directly arrest anyone in Japan. But I can ID the killer and get the cops to act. Of course, I have the rights to do that."

"Then…"

"I can't promise you I'll catch them, but I'll do my best to try. At least, as long as I'm alive," I said.

Gamon looked a little relieved. "You're exaggerating, Asunyan."

"I told you not to call me that."

"I-I'm sorry."

Was he making fun of me because I looked like a little girl? It honestly felt like he was just trying to make me mad.

"Oh, um. Thanks. Kizaki."

"It's fine. She was a student at my school, too. Even if we never met."

An "exaggeration," huh?

As long as I'm alive…

I wasn't exaggerating. I'd meant it. I didn't have a lot of time left. Of course, there was no reason I had to explain that to Gamon.

"By the way, why do you think there are two of my Skysensors?" Gamon pointed, confused, at his radio, which was now slung on my shoulder. "I mean, I've got one, too." He showed me the one that was on his shoulder.

They both looked exactly the same. They even had the same

anime character strap attached to the base of the shoulder belt.

"Can I touch it?" Gamon reached out with shaking hands toward the radio I was holding.

"Can ghosts touch things?" I asked, just as his fingers touched the radio.

No, I couldn't tell if he touched it or if his hands went through it. The second his fingers reached it, I was shocked to see the one on his shoulder disappear, bag and all.

"What...?"

There was no flash of light or anything, like out of a fairy tale. It simply vanished in an instant, without a sound. As if it had never existed...

But Gamon himself didn't even notice.

"Yuta Gamon, where's your radio?"

"Huh? H-huh?" Only when I told him did he realize. He frantically looked around for it. "Wait... where is it? Where did my Skysensor go?!"

This was another bizarre thing I'd just witnessed.

Moritsuka, what's going on in this town? I asked silently. No, Gamon was a ghost, so trying to use normal logic on him was a waste of time to begin with. At least, that's what I tried to tell myself. If I didn't, I might start panicking like he was. "It disappeared."

"It disappeared? What do you mean?!"

"Don't ask me."

Both Gamon and I sat there in silence, staring at the spot on his shoulder where the radio had disappeared. Of course, no matter how long we waited, the radio didn't come back.

Gamon's shoulders slumped. Maybe he'd given up.

"Listen." He turned towards me with a serious expression. "Can you turn on the power on the radio you've got?"

"Why?"

"I want to see if it's broken or not. It's something that reminds me of my dad."

I nodded, had him tell me which of the many switches on the radio to flip, and turned the power on.

—Zzzzzz zzzzzz

Static began to pour out from the speaker. It had sunk into a lake once already, so it must have been pretty sturdily built.

"Good, it's not broken." Gamon stared at the radio with a look of relief. As the anger he'd displayed when I brought up his parents suggested, he really cared about his family.

"Has anybody but your dad ever held this radio for a long time?"

Gamon seemed confused at my question. "What do you mean?"

"I just used my psychometry on this radio. And there was a weird girl's voice."

"A-a weird girl's voice? Zonko, maybe?"

"What? Who's Zonko?"

"Sometimes this radio just starts talking. In a girl's voice. It's really bratty and always tells me to do things."

What was he talking about? No, I couldn't use common sense on Gamon. I just couldn't. He was dead.

"Who is this Zonko girl, though?"

"Her." Gamon pointed at the character strap tied to the radio. "*MMM*'s Zonko."

"An anime character?"

"That's right. *Master Mast Murder.*"

"And it talks?"

"Oh, no. The radio talks, and it felt to me like it was Zonko talking. So I just decided to call it Zonko."

My head was starting to hurt again. I had no idea what he was saying.

I decided to stop listening to Gamon and use my psychometry again. I told Gamon to sit back down in his chair, took off my glove, and touched the radio. I did the same performance as I'd done before.

"I'm sorry."

There it was again. I could hear it, and…

Something seemed strange about what I was seeing after Gamon sank into the water. I took a closer look.

The moon was flickering on the surface of the water, and deep within its light, I could see another image. That's how it felt.

This happened sometimes when I read memories. It was probably particularly strong memories from another temporal axis leaking out onto this one.

What time were the memories from? I focused my mind on tracking it down. It was like finding a thin thread and following it. Given how exhausted I was, it wasn't something I really wanted to do.

I found it. Once I identified the time, all I had to do was rewind and play it.

The movie screen showed a small room, a microphone, and an audio console covered with buttons and instruments. It was the same thing I'd seen when I touched the booth's microphone a moment ago. These were memories of when Yuta Gamon's father,

Koresuke Gamon, was still alive.

There was a mirror in front of him, and I could see his reflection. He was sitting in front of the microphone, reading from what seemed to be a script. He looked like a very kind man. He looked very plain, not at all like my image of a pro radio DJ. Outside the window, a young Yuta Gamon was staring at him, eyes shining.

But then I realized something was strange. Something was different from when I'd used my psychometry on the microphone before.

What was it?

I stared at the image on the projector, carefully observing it.

"What's this?" There was a window in the studio facing outside, and reflected in it was another stream of images.

An image leaking out from a leaking image? That had never happened before. A warning bell rang in my mind, but the memories wanted to speak to me. I had to see them.

I went deeper within the memories.

The new memory was at roughly the same point in time as what I'd just seen in the recording studio. However, this was completely different.

It was a fairly large room, like some kind of meeting hall. In one corner of the hall was a pile of backpacks and bags. The radio must have been lying on the pile, because my field of vision was tilted.

The room had no windows and was dimly lit. The only source of light was a ritual fire from the back of the room. At first I couldn't tell because of the dark, but there were more people in the room than I'd thought. Everyone was wearing eerie masks and shaking their bodies from side to side.

Was this…a ritual?

Just then, someone ran up to the man in white robes who was sitting closest to the fire. The man who ran up was the only one not wearing a mask. It was the man I'd just seen in the DJ booth—Koresuke Gamon. He grabbed the man in white by the collar and violently lifted him up, but then all the others wearing the masks rose and charged, piling on him.

Suddenly, the screen began to flicker. By the time I realized something was wrong, my mind had been pulled back to reality.

"Gaahh!" My heart felt like it was being squeezed like a dishrag. I couldn't even breathe. I just held my chest and endured the pain.

I have to catch my breath, I thought, but it was beyond a level I could control. All the blood vessels in my body were on fire, and the flames threatened to burn my body to ash. The pain overwhelmed me, and I started to pass out. Just when I thought I was done for…

"Hey! Wake up!" Gamon grabbed me by the shoulders and shook me violently.

It was enough to barely wake me up. I gritted my teeth to endure the pain. My tote bag was right next to me. There were painkiller capsules inside. If I took some…

I rummaged through the tote bag with shaking fingers. Gamon helped me.

"This?" He found the pill case I was looking for. I nodded and he took out a capsule from the case.

I put it in my mouth and desperately swallowed it, then closed my eyes. I tensed up my body for a while and endured the pain. Gamon took out a bottle of mineral water from my bag and offered it to me, so I took a sip.

After fifteen minutes or so, the pain stopped.

"*Hahh...hahh...*" That was close. I was lucky I'd survived.

"Are you okay now?"

"Yeah. Thanks." I caught my breath and took another sip of water.

I'd been using my psychometry constantly since I'd gone back to being an investigator. It had taken a bigger toll on me than I'd thought. If I didn't cut back on using my power, I'd be in real danger.

"Kizaki, are you sick?" Gamon asked. He'd been watching over me the whole time, trying to see if there was anything he could do to help.

"Don't worry about it. It's got nothing to do with you." I stood up from my chair. I looked at my phone and saw that I'd missed a call from Shinoyama. Maybe something had happened. It was time to go back to the station. "If I ever want to contact you in the future, what do I do?"

"Hmm, go to Café Blue Moon. Sarai and Toko are there, too." He seemed to know a lot of people.

"Are they like you?"

"There's no other useless NEET like me out there. Sorry."

"That's not what I meant. Do they still have their memories of when they were alive and are living out their normal lives?"

"Yeah, that's right."

"What are they like?"

"One's an editor at *Mumuu*. Then there're Basara Girls One and Two, I guess. Also, the son of Dr. Hashigami. He's smart, and he loves to prove people wrong, but that's all he's good for. Oh, and he's in college."

"Answer me seriously."

"I am answering you seriously. Everything I just said is true. If you come, you'll understand."

They sounded like a bunch of weirdos. Then...

"Are any of your friends a detective?"

"A detective? Oh, come to think of it, there was a weird detective in a trench coat I talked to a little after I died."

"What? Is that true?!" I grabbed Gamon without thinking. "What's his name?! Was it Moritsuka?"

Gamon nodded, a little scared.

"Where is he now?!"

"I-I don't know. I only ever met him once."

Oh wow... so Moritsuka was in the same state Gamon was in. Then would I someday be able to speak to him, like I could speak to Gamon?

"I'm sorry for grabbing you. Moritsuka was the person in charge of this case before me. If you see him, tell him about me."

"I-I don't know if I'll see him again."

"Please."

Gamon nodded a little. "Oh, don't forget about the interview," he said. "A Japanese FBI High School Hot Girl Psychometer is sure to pull in a lot of hits."

Hits. I wished he'd stop calling me by that long title.

Then suddenly, Gamon sighed deeply and started reading the letters on the walls with a sad expression. On the surface, he seemed to be doing well, but maybe it was just an act. He'd seen his own body yesterday. It would make sense.

"Yuta Gamon. I'm glad I got to talk to you," I said. "I want to believe there's a reason we met like this."

It was because of the hint Moritsuka had left me. If he had left it for me, there had to be a reason. If I could gain information from the 256 people who'd died, maybe it would help me solve the case.

Or maybe I was just hallucinating. If I was, Shinoyama would notice and send me to the hospital. If that happened, then fine. For now, I would just do what I could.

"Maybe it's irresponsible to say this, but… There are things you can do because of who you are now. Thank you for your help. If I need something, I'll come to you."

There was nothing else I could say to him. Gamon and I could speak to one another, but we weren't the same. There was a cold, unbridgeable difference that separated us.

The living, and the dead. Even if the line was a thin one, the places we stood were very far apart. He could never go back to where I was.

That's why I parted with him then.

PARANORMAL SCIENCE NVL

Occultic;Nine

オカルティック・ナイン

THERE IS NO SUCH THING AS THE "OCCULT." IT CAN ALL BE DISPROVED BY SCIENCE.
ONLY THOSE WHO HAVE ACCEPTED EVERYTHING
HAVE THE RIGHT TO KNOW THE TRUTH.

▶ site 73: Toko Sumikaze

I headed to work from Gotanda Station, got into the elevator from the front hall, and got off at the editors' floor.

Until now, no matter how tired or exhausted I'd been when I arrived, I'd done most of my work automatically. Now, if I didn't carefully think about everything I was doing, the fear threatened to overwhelm me. Even the office I'd seen a million times before was starting to feel like another world.

I got out of the elevator, took a deep breath to slow my heart rate, and entered the editorial department.

"Good evening!" I said, in a louder voice than I really needed to.

Nobody answered. I looked around and saw that none of my co-workers were sitting at their desks. Had everybody gone home at the end of the work day? There were still several days before the final deadline for the magazine, but it was rare to have absolutely nobody here.

Just—

"I see… nobody's here, huh?" I felt a little relieved to realize it.

"Ascension… maybe I'm a little weaker than I thought." Not that it really mattered at this point.

Yesterday, I'd gone to Daiseiji and seen my own corpse. I'd seen my own dead body with my own two eyes. It was hard, just like I thought it would be. My job was working with the occult, and I'd always been able to sense "ghosts" near me, so I thought that would give me some strength to endure it.

"I guess I'm in no position to laugh at Gamon, huh?" When I was with him and the other kids, I'd been trying my best to stay calm because I was older, but I'd actually been as scared as them.

I headed to my desk and sat down in the beat-up chair, then sighed and stretched out my legs. Just then, I saw a paper bag under the desk. "Isn't this…?"

Inside the bag were about twenty books. They were the ones I'd borrowed after Dr. Hashigami had recommended them to me.

"Doctor… I'm sorry I never got to give them back to you." I thought of the man whose face I would never see and whose voice I would never hear, and put my hands together.

What would I do with these? I was dead now, but I needed to give them back to Dr. Hashigami's family. Maybe I'd give them to Sarai.

"But I doubt he'd really appreciate it." What should I do with them?

Wait, didn't I have more important problems to deal with? Why was I wasting my mental energy on this stuff? I sighed again just as I heard a voice out in the hall.

"Yes…yes, everything's going according to plan. It's fine. Yes… I'm very grateful to the Hachifukushin Circle… the money's coming in fine... yes... yes..." The editor-in-chief came into the room, his phone pressed to his ear.

I stood up without thinking. I'd been caught off guard, and I'd tensed up. Would he be able to see me? Or...

I steeled myself and waved once I was sure I was in his field of vision. When I'd done this before, he'd always glanced at me quickly and then waved back.

He didn't even look at me as he went straight to his seat.

"S-sir!" I yelled. My voice echoed throughout the small room—or at least it should have, but the editor-in-chief didn't respond at all. Normally, even if you wanted to ignore someone, a loud yell like that would startle you. "He can't hear me."

Thinking back, that morning when the bodies had been pulled out of Inokashira Lake, something had seemed wrong when I'd talked to the editor-in-chief and the rest of my co-workers as we watched the news.

So that was it. They couldn't see or hear me.

"Ascension, right?" Suddenly I felt dizzy. I grabbed my desk to keep from falling to the floor. It was no good. If I stayed here any longer, the reality of the situation was going to crush me. I went to stagger out of the room.

"Yes... Dr. Hashigami's essay... at some point... as planned..."

Did he just say Dr. Hashigami? The editor-in-chief was still talking to someone on the phone. He sounded very serious, and his voice was a whisper even though nobody else was here.

What was this feeling? My intuition as a *Mumuu* reporter was picking up something. I turned around and went back to his desk.

"Yes... all right... thank you. Goodbye." He bowed his head

several times and finally hung up the phone. He put away his phone and stretched out his limbs. He seemed annoyed. "*Sigh*... those people are just obnoxious. They do pay pretty well, though."

He didn't even notice that I was right in front of him. His eyes were turned toward the laptop on his desk.

I walked around behind him without the slightest fear of being discovered and looked at the computer screen. "Ascension!"

The screen was showing an essay by Dr. Hashigami. It was a scanned PDF with his personal signature on the front page.

It was dated February 11th?

"What is this?"

I'd never seen it before. I'd been in charge of checking all the essays Dr. Hashigami wrote for *Mumuu*. So how was there one I'd never seen before, and from the 11th of February...?

"That's the day he went missing!"

That would mean this was his last essay! Why did the editor-in-chief have this? The title of the essay on the monitor was...

"Time and the Spiritualizing World"

▶ **site 74: MMG**

"Currently, the synchronization rate with the human world is ninety-seven percent and stable, and harmonics and all other values are within normal parameters. This result is beyond what we expected, and even I'm a little surprised. Of course, there are no major bugs being reported in the logic analyzer now that it's in actual use. Since Nikola Tesla's system is 8-bit, though, there is a question of how much modern technology we'll be able to incorporate into it."

The rows of men leaned forward, eager to hear what Takasu had to say. They were looking at the data on the big screen above his head and muttering to themselves.

"These wonderful numbers are a direct result of Dr. Hashigami's unpublished paper, 'Time and the Spiritualizing World.' After acquiring the paper, we gave it a detailed analysis and succeeded in solving the problems we had with synchronizing with absolute time. It's no exaggeration to say that he is the man responsible for the creation of the New World System. His loss was a great one."

"It was a very occultic incident, wasn't it?" Hatoyama joked, and the rest of them let out a dry laugh.

Even Takasu curled his lips up into a slight grin and shrugged a little. "There are some things in the world it's better not to learn too much about."

"So, what about the bugs reported during the first phase?" Matoba raised a hand to get the discussion back on track.

"There's no issue with that, either. Even after the second phase began, we've continued our tracking, but there was a great difference in the amount of scandium in each. Of course, we've upped the sensitivity and are continuing to track the orphan receptors, but even if a signal surpasses base values, that is, if anything, evidence that the synchronization values are increasing."

"Then the second phase is a success, too?"

"Yes, it was." Takasu nodded.

"Which means at this very instant, the 256 astral bodies are synchronized to the same absolute time that we are?" Now it was Hatoyama's turn to ask a question.

"Correct. At this point, it's simply a question of whether you have a body, or not. The synchronization of the spiritual and human worlds has brought our New World System to the level of actual use."

The men smiled, satisfied with his words. The several-months-long delay had only made their desire to hear of the system's completion stronger.

"Is the report on our success ready, then? It will make the business discussions go far easier."

"I'll explain the New World System's business plan once more,"

Takasu answered, and the data on the big screen disappeared, replaced by the logo of the Bavarian Illuminati and the term "New World System."

"In every era, it's been mostly the rich and those with high positions in society, like company heads, who have wanted eternal life. And we will sell them the New World System, where we inject them with scandium and bathe them in special electromagnetic waves to make that possible. Even if their body dies, their personality and memories will remain. That is what they want. And by offering them their heart's desire, we will be able to climb to a position greater than they had possessed in life."

As Takasu spoke, images of microchips appeared on the large screen. "The microchip plan. The plan to control human society by implanting everyone with chips was one recognized by even Rockefeller, but in addition to the cost and risk, issues with the implantation process made it impossible to realize. And so—"

An image of the alpha-type scandium isotope appeared on the screen. "We turned our attention to scandium. This material, which is used in everything from fuel cells to ICBMs, is extremely versatile. Microscopic scandium, preloaded with information, has little effect on the human body and can even be injected into newborn babies in some cases. Once it's administered via any method except orally, it passes from the blood to the brain, where it takes over the corpus callosum and can never be removed. It's expensive, but allows us extremely low-risk human guinea pigs."

The video on the screen displayed a simple, easy-to-understand diagram of scandium multiplying once it was inside a human body.

"Scandium is highly responsive, both in terms of electrical

resistance rate and magnetism, so it has no choice but to respond with a high degree of sensitivity to the EM waves put out by the New World System. In other words, we can transmit our orders directly to the brains of recipients."

Hatoyama interrupted. "Don't forget that that's why we went forward with plans for terrestrial HD broadcasting, to free up the analog spectrum."

"We're very grateful to the government for their help with that." Takasu smiled at the proud Hatoyama and continued. "I'm sure you understand this already, but we're going to sell the New World System to the wealthy and elite with promises of eternal life. And then we'll be able to control the minds of everyone who purchased it. By controlling the elite, we'll be able to develop an incredibly lucrative business at no risk whatsoever. And…we'll be able to do it forever."

The men broke into applause.

"Amazing."

"Truly, a wonderful plan."

The somber, dimly lit room was swept with a strange fever.

Even Takasu himself was a little flush with his success. "Now then…"

Takasu coughed once as a signal to stop the applause. Several photos and profiles appeared on the screen. It was a list of the most important figures in Japan's political and business world.

"We already have reservations for the first 150 people who want to use the scandium required for the New World System. Eternal Life is a very compelling product."

One of the seated men—Matoba—spoke up. "One hundred

million yen for the scandium. Twenty million yen yearly for an administration fee. Multiply that by 150 people, huh? Not a bad start."

"Some people have too much money. Just what you'd expect from the chosen people." Hatoyama had told several jokes today, making it clear that he was in a better mood than usual. "Running the business through the Hachifukushin Circle was a good decision. If we make it look like people in dire need of salvation have donated huge amounts of money to a religious organization, no one will blame them."

"So the religion is a cloak to hide our true intentions? Clever."

"Takasu here is one of the leading figures in Japanese medicine. It's not the sort of idea you'd expect him to come up with."

Takasu grinned when he heard that. "The final goal of medicine is to reach a place beyond the death of the body. I am simply seeking to take medicine to its final frontier."

And then...

Suddenly, the list on the screen was erased, and the symbol of the Bavarian Illuminati appeared on the screen. A voice, clearly different than Takasu or the other men's, filled the room.

"The final frontier of medicine, huh?"

Everyone in the room froze. Then, they all stood up from their chairs. As the tension in the room rose, they all bowed their heads in the direction of the screen.

Of course, Takasu did as well. He lowered his head and stared at the floor. It felt to him like the temperature of the room had dropped several degrees.

"Master!" Even Takasu could barely keep his voice from shaking.

The master of the Bavarian Illuminati. The man who had controlled Japan's medical world ever since the end of the war. A living legend who had created all the plans that Takasu and the others were advancing.

That was the person Takasu called "Master."

"Takasu, what is the final frontier of medicine that you seek?" The voice was flat and monotone, and a normal person would have found it strange.

There was a strange static mixed in with it, as if a machine, not a human, were speaking.

Takasu tensed his whole body as he spoke, the complete opposite of the easygoing way he'd spoken to the men a moment ago. "If medicine so far has been the struggle against death and disease, then isn't accepting even death and rising to something beyond it the final frontier of medicine... the ultimate salvation?"

There was a pause, and then the voice spoke again. "Then you think that saving people is a good deed?"

"Yes," Takasu said, still looking at the floor.

"You're wrong."

Surprised, Takasu shivered.

The voice continued. "Saving lives that should die and souls that should be destroyed, in violation of the laws of nature... that is an unforgivable act of blasphemy that goes against the source of life formed by the Sephirotic Tree. However, this 'evil' is what has advanced society and brought the world to the future. In other words...'evil' is the final frontier of medicine."

▶ site 75: Yuta Gamon

Toko had told me she had something she wanted to talk to me about, so I headed to Café Blue Moon. As I walked through the hotel section on the way from the station to the café, Sarai called out to me from behind.

He walked up alongside me. "Where did you go yesterday?"

If he meant after we'd met at Daiseiji, I'd gone home and cried... but I couldn't tell Sarai that. So I said nothing.

Oh, but maybe I should tell him about Asunyan. Before I could decide what to say, he began to talk.

"I looked to see if there was anyone else we knew at Daiseiji."

"Huh? Seriously? Man, you're tough. Or are you some kind of monster?"

"Are you insulting me?"

"I just...I just don't know how you could do that and stay calm."

"It wasn't easy, even for me. But panicking won't help solve anything."

Man, maybe he really *was* tough.

"And?"

"I found Aikawa."

"...Yeah."

"And the mistress of the House of Crimson."

"Aria Kurenaino? I see..."

The incident at Enmeiji was after the 256 Incident. We'd been able to talk with Aria when she visited Blue Moon, so it made sense that she was dead.

"Also, I don't know if it's the same person... but there was also the body of a girl named Ririka Nishizono."

"Huh, really?!" Ririka Nishizono, the one who'd drawn the manga that had foretold what happened?

"If I remember right, I met her once at school. We didn't really talk, though."

"If she's dead, does that mean she doesn't have anything to do with Dr. Hashigami's death?"

"I don't know. There's no way to be sure it's even the same Ririka Nishizono who drew the manga."

"Y-you're right..."

Even so, a lot of people I knew were dead. Two hundred fifty-six people who either lived, worked, or went to school in Kichijoji... It felt like the odds of me knowing anybody would be pretty low.

Was it just a coincidence that so many names I knew were included? Or... was there some reason?

Asunyan said that my father was involved somehow in the 256 Incident, and so was I. Was something happening around me?

"By the way, Narusawa wasn't there," Sarai added.

"Huh? Really?" Did that mean Ryotasu wasn't dead? Then that meant that just like Asunyan, she could see and talk to me even though she was alive, huh? "What about Master Izumin?"

"I don't even know his real name. There was no way to look."

"Oh, I see. But you should be able to tell once you see his body, right? He's so creepy—I mean, distinctive."

"You're right. I didn't see any bodies like that."

In other words, Ryotasu and Master Izumin weren't victims of the 256 Incident. Both were alive.

"I see. They're...alive."

I didn't care so much about Master Izumin, but I wanted to be happy that Ryotasu was alive... yet somehow, it wasn't that easy. After all, I was dead.

"It may be too early to be sure. All we know for a fact is that her body wasn't there."

"What about the list of victims? Shouldn't they have everybody ID'd by now?"

If Ryotasu's name wasn't on it, that would settle it.

"There are still about twenty people who haven't been identified. We should look again."

The conversation ended there.

Sarai and I headed to the café, walking side-by-side. Walking like this with Sarai was somehow kind of...

"I'd rather walk next to a pretty girl."

"Huh? What are you talking about?"

"Nothing." I fell silent again.

There was probably no reason I had to force myself to talk to Sarai, but...

When I was with Ryotasu, I had no trouble talking, so what was different now?

"Hey Sarai, what do you think about psychometers?"

"Psychometers?"

"Um, there's a type of psychic power where you can touch something and read the memories it has—"

"I know that. It's stupid. Memories, in objects? How are objects going to have memories when they don't have an organ that functions like a brain? The 'memories' are just a fantasy dreamed up by the psychometer."

"I thought you'd say that."

"So why are you asking?"

"W-well, I met this girl who's a hot Japanese high school girl who's also a psychometer FBI agent..."

If I introduced her to Sarai, they'd probably have a big fight. Would Sarai win? Or would Asunyan use her powers to prove him wrong?

Damn. That would be really interesting. It would be like those TV programs they used to do where they'd test psychics. If I put together something like that on Kirikiri Basara, it would be a big hit.

"If you want to talk about manga, talk to Narusawa, not me." Sarai said.

Grr...just you wait. Soon I'll introduce you to Asunyan, and you'll see who's boss!

Eventually, we reached Café Blue Moon. Toko was there, and she told us what happened at the *Mumuu* office.

"My dad... Dr. Hashigami... had another essay?"

"Yes. And it was finished on February eleventh."

"That's the day my dad went missing!" Sarai gasped.

"It's possible my editor-in-chief is involved with his murder, isn't it?" Toko took off her glasses and rubbed her eyelids with her thumbs. She wore a subdued expression. "There was one time he went to get a draft from the doctor without saying anything to me. I did think that was strange."

"What do you mean?"

"Going to get the draft was my job. That was the only time he ever did it."

"When was this?"

"I just checked in my notebook. February sixteenth."

"That's after my dad had gone missing."

Dr. Hashigami had died on February twenty-fourth. That's the day I'd gone to his lab, and—

"My dad died on the twenty-fourth. On that day, somebody raided his study."

"So it was possible the editor-in-chief got into the study before then and took the draft." Toko snapped her fingers. "It was probably something different from what he planned to run in the magazine. It was way too big to fit his column length."

"Maybe it was the culmination of my father's research, then?" Sarai shivered a little.

"Um," I raised my hand timidly. "Why did *Mumuu*'s editor-in-chief have to take the draft?"

"The obvious answer is that somebody didn't want it getting published."

"But it's weird that the *Mumuu* editor-in-chief is involved, then."

Of course, this was still a guess.

"But think about it. What if *Mumuu* was controlling information? What if they were making sure all the information that got out was stuff normal people wouldn't believe in order to trick people? And then they kept the truth hidden… you could have a hypothesis like that, couldn't you?" Toko said.

Toko was a *Mumuu* editor, too. Did she realize how impossible most of the stuff she wrote sounded? But…

"It smells like a conspiracy!"

Normally this was where Sarai would jump in to prove us wrong, but he just bit his lip and clenched his fists. He was being emotional, for once. It looked like he was trying his best to keep his emotions in check with rationality.

Sarai sighed and took out his phone, making notes with incredible speed.

"I understand the situation. Let's go over all this." By the time he was done writing, Sarai was back to his usual self. "Sumikaze, do you know what was in the paper your boss was hiding?"

"Yes." Toko nodded. "He hid the USB memory stick it was on right in front of me. I still can't believe that his Easter Island statue had a gimmick like that. No, actually that's more like something I would expect from him."

So she'd been able to find his secret because she was a ghost? It was the same thing I'd done when I went to peek into the bath. I wondered if we could do some kind of detective routine. We could make Ryotasu the actual detective while Sarai and I solved the crimes. Like some kind of Arthur Conan Doyle thing.

"I copied the data onto my phone."

"Huh, wait a second. Toko, you were able to touch that USB stick?"

"What do you mean?"

"No, just… We're dead, and like ghosts, right? Can we touch physical objects?"

"That's a good point…" Toko's eyebrows furrowed. "But I was able to touch it just fine. I was even able to use the PC."

"Oh…"

That's right. I'd done plenty of updates on Kirikiri Basara. I was a ghost, but I could still use the laptop.

Toko took out her phone and showed me the screen. It was a PDF of a handwritten draft. Dr. Hashigami's handwriting covered the page.

"The title is 'Time and the Spiritualizing World.' This was my father's last essay…" Sarai took more notes with his phone. That seemed to be how he was trying to maintain his calm. "Can you upload it to the Cloud? I'll be able to download it then."

Toko used her phone to start uploading the data.

"So was there anything else you noticed? You said he was talking on the phone. Who was he talking to?"

"I don't know. But he said the name of some weird group."

"Group?"

Toko nodded and gave me the name. "The Hachifukushin Circle."

"What?!" That name! I was so stunned that for a moment I forgot to breathe.

"Gamon, you know it?"

"Kn-know it? I just heard it from someone else today."

My father's secret, which Asunyan had told me about. "It's an organization my dad belonged to… I guess."

"What did you say?"

What was going on here? The dots were starting to connect, and it was my dad who connected them. An ordinary guy who'd died seven years ago. An ordinary guy who'd just happened to have his own mini-FM radio station.

He was kind, and gentle. He often suffered because of that, but at least he wasn't the type of person to trick people or hurt them. That had always been how I'd thought of my dad.

Today, though, that image was falling apart.

"That… that can't be true."

"It doesn't mean everything happened because your father wanted it to."

Suddenly, someone whispered in my ear from behind me, and I jumped up. It was a man with a young-looking face, wearing a trench coat and a cap.

"Oh! It's the cosplaying detective!" When did he get here? I hadn't even seen him come into the café!

Detective Moritsuka smiled. "Hello there. It's me, Zenigata! Just kidding. By the way, this isn't cosplay." He took off his cap and bowed. "Moritsuka, with the Musashino Police. Not Morizuka; Moritsuka. Nice to meet you."

Toko and Sarai bowed back, obviously confused.

"You're dead too, right? Asu—the high school girl FBI investigator—was worried about you."

"Was she?" Moritsuka whispered her name and looked sad. But that was only for a moment, and he quickly went back to his normal, faint smile. Then he put his hand on my shoulder, a little too friendly for my liking. "Can you tell her not to push herself too hard if you see her? Thanks."

"So you do know her."

"Yeah, I guess." Moritsuka stepped away from me and began to twirl his cap with his fingers. "Still, she's already found out all that about the Hachifukushin Circle? Pretty impressive."

Asunyan said that Moritsuka had been in charge of the case before she was. She was investigating the hints that he'd left. So maybe he knew something about my dad and the case that I didn't. From what I knew about him, there was no way he'd just tell me.

"How much do you know, and about what?" Sarai asked Moritsuka warily.

"Tch-tch-tch. Don't make too many assumptions about me." Moritsuka didn't answer. He always talked like this. "There isn't much I know. Making it seem like you know more than you do and upsetting the person you talk to are both interrogation techniques. Scare them or make them mad, and they'll tell you things they didn't intend to."

"Grr…"

He was so right I couldn't do anything but groan.

"The thing is, though, we don't have a lot of time. If we want to take action, it's best that we hurry."

PARANORMAL SCIENCE NVL

Occultic;Nine

オカルティック・ナイン

THERE IS NO SUCH THING AS THE "OCCULT." IT CAN ALL BE DISPROVED BY SCIENCE.
ONLY THOSE WHO HAVE ACCEPTED EVERYTHING
HAVE THE RIGHT TO KNOW THE TRUTH.

▶ site 76: Miyuu Aikawa

"If you don't like it, you can always quit. So give it a try!"

It was that proposal of Chi's that had made me start livestreaming.

My dad, the only one who'd told me that my power wasn't wrong, had died, and ever since then I'd avoided telling fortunes for other people. I'd only use my power on myself. Even if the results were bad, they would only be bad for me.

The future never changed because of my fortune-telling. That's what I'd thought.

That's how I'd lived, until one day Chi had said, "Don't be afraid. Try telling other people's fortunes. Prove that your dad didn't die because of your fortune-telling. It'll be fine! I'll be right there with you!"

Her words had given me courage.

After that, Chi had worked as hard as she could to get ready. She found out how to livestream on Nico and negotiated with the teachers to get permission to use the AV room at school.

She'd even hand-made the decorations we used in the room for the performance.

She was the first person whose fortune I'd told on my livestream. It was a demonstration where I guessed the cards that Chi flipped over. One of the listeners had thought it was neat, and called in. That was how my fortune-telling program got its start.

Barely anybody watched at first. Nobody insulted me, but nobody praised me, either. At that early stage, Chi was the only regular viewer. Sometimes the microphone would pick up Chi laughing. At the end of the program, sometimes listeners would say, "Say hi to your helper for us!" too.

One day I'd invited her to come in front of the camera. *"I'm fine. This is your broadcast, Myu,"* she'd said.

She'd laughed and turned me down. If I'd been asked, though, I'd have said this program was both of ours.

The first time I got a mean comment, Chi was madder than I was. When I was upgraded from a user stream to an official stream, Chi was happier than anybody.

A week after that had been Chi's birthday. After a lot of thought, I'd finally settled on a really cute hairpiece with a little cartoon dog on it. It was made by an amateur, and I'd found it at a crafts fair. The dog's droopy eyes and bothered expression were so cute, and somehow it reminded me of Chi.

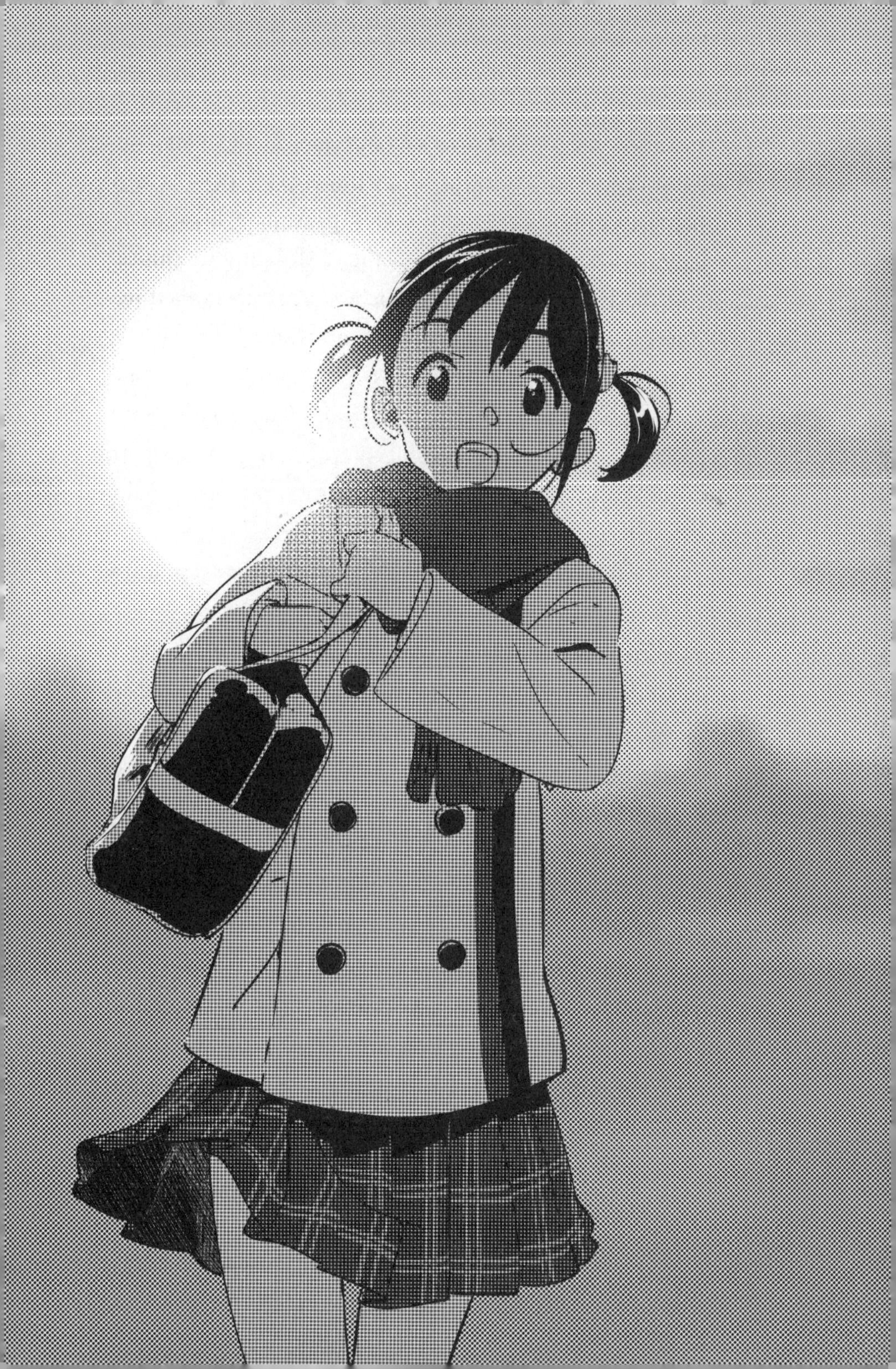

I told her that when I gave it to her, and she'd laughed happily.

"Okay, you can wear it during your livestreams, then," she'd said. "When something sad happens or something bothers you, pretend you're thinking and touch it, and then cheer up! I'll always, always be there for you!" She'd tried the hairpiece on right then, then took it off and put it on my head.

I was happy. I remember I almost cried.

I was only able to keep livestreaming because of you, Chi.

The feelings of gratitude almost brought me to tears. I suddenly closed my eyes tight.

"Does it look good on me?" I heard Chi say.

I opened my eyes, trying to keep from crying, and went to nod...

On top of the desk in front of me was a red lump of meat.

On top of the smashed meat was a hairpiece with a cartoon dog.

The dog's eyes, stained red, were staring right at me.

"Aaaaaaaaaaaaaaaah!" I opened my eyes and saw the ceiling of my room. The lights were off.

The spring sunlight was pouring in past the closed curtains.

I realized I was holding something. I looked and saw it was a hairpiece with a cartoon dog on it.

I was at home. I was in my room. Nobody was home but me.

I hadn't let in any air, and the curtains had been closed all day, so the air in the room was musty. I must have been sleeping again.

I slept and got up, spaced out for a while, and then slept again. I wasn't sure how many days I'd been repeating that cycle. It just felt like if I stayed here, Chi would open the door and come right in.

"Chi..." I called the name of my dear friend in a voice hoarse from sobbing.

She'd say, "Myu, are you okay?" and then I'd give her a big hug and tell her I had a scary dream and cry. Then Chi would probably pat my head and tell me it was okay. She was shorter than me, but she liked to pretend she was an older sister.

I kept hoping it would happen, but my door never moved an inch.

With nothing else to do, I stood up from the bed and opened the curtains. It was so bright outside. There wasn't a cloud in the whole sky. It was the perfect day to go outside.

I hated it.

"I want a crepe…"

When I'd gone with Chi to get crepes, I'd always decide what I wanted before I got in line, but then when I got to the point where I ordered, I would always change my mind. Chi liked hers simple, with sugar and butter, or honey and butter. I liked the ones packed with cream and fruit.

We didn't have the money to buy a lot of them, and they had a ton of calories, so we'd only order one for both of us to share. That meant either Chi or I had to give up on the one we liked. We'd try to settle on something, until finally Chi would pick the one I liked, and we would split it and eat it together.

I would never be able to eat crepes with Chi again. Just thinking that made me cry once more.

"Chi!" I sobbed and yelled her name, knowing she would never hear me, and then…

The phone on my pillow started to vibrate, as if in answer to my voice.

I gasped in surprise and stared at it. The vibration quickly stopped. For several days now, I hadn't had the energy to answer the phone, but this time I wanted to know who it was.

Trembling, I reached out my hand for the LCD screen and tapped it with my fingertip.

The light from the screen was so bright. I peered down at it.

When I saw the name, I couldn't look away.

"Chi."

≫ STEINS;GATE

A visual novel published in 2009 for the Xbox 360. It was later ported to other systems and turned into an anime and a stage play as well.

≫ UDX

A high-rise building in front of Akihabara station. It has twenty-two floors. The first six floors contain meeting rooms, event spaces, mini theaters, etc. The seventh floor and higher are offices.

≫ CAGLIOSTRO'S CASTLE

The name of the castle in the anime film *Lupin III: The Castle of Cagliostro*.

≫ BACKSTAGE PASS

Official name: "AKIHABARA Backstage Pass." An idol-training entertainment café in Akihabara. The concept is that it's a fictional idol talent agency, and the over one hundred female staff are called the "Idol Cast," who sing and dance on the stage in the café every day. Customers are producers who can "produce" (vote) for the girls of their choice, and rankings are published monthly. Some members of the cast go on to put out CDs or appear on TV programs.

≫ Q.E.D

Latin for "Quod Erat Demonstrandum," which means "Thus it has been demonstrated." Put at the completion of mathematical or philosophical proofs. It is almost never used today.

≫ BLACK THUNDER

A chocolate candy that was first sold in Japan in 1994. Its catchphrase is "Popular with young girls!" Also exists as ice cream, with many limited-time versions.

≫ MATRYOSHKA DOLL

A traditional Russian craft. A hollow doll with a smaller doll inside, which then contains an even smaller doll. Sometimes, there can be five or six dolls inside the first one.

≫ KISARAGI STATION

An urban legend that originated on 2ch. Kisaragi Station doesn't exist, but people will occasionally make real-time posts about how they've "gotten lost there." The real-time nature of the posts makes them especially realistic and horrifying.

≫ FARIS-TAN

The name of a character in *Steins;Gate*. A cat-eared maid who works in an Akihabara maid café, a.k.a. Faris NyanNyan.

≫ FM-KCZ

A local mini-FM radio station run by Yuta's father. It hasn't been active since his death seven years ago. A mini-FM radio station is even smaller in scale than a community-FM radio station and is sometimes called Micro-FM. It's not considered a broadcasting station under the law, so it doesn't require a license.

≫ THIS IS SNAKE

A line spoken by Snake, the hero of the game *Metal Gear Solid*. Snake is a character who specializes in infiltration, and so it's used online to indicate that someone has identified a home or workplace which is currently the subject of a controversy and actually visited it.

≫ EL PSY KONGROO

A phrase of unknown meaning spoken by Rintaro Okabe, the protagonist of *Steins;Gate*. According to him, it's a goodbye, but the origin is unknown.

≫ ROCKEFELLER

One of America's richest families. The Oil King John D. Rockefeller brought them vast wealth, and eventually they came to have enormous influence. The Rockefellers, Morgans, and Mellons are said to be America's three most powerful families.

≫ DR. DUNCAN MACDOUGALL

An American doctor. 1866-1920. He did experiments to determine the weight of a soul, and it was from him that the theory that a soul weighs twenty-one grams spread. However, this theory is not recognized scientifically.

≫ FBI

The acronym for the Federal Bureau of Investigation, an American law enforcement organization. It is a part of the Department of Justice, with approximately 30,000 employees. It investigates violations of federal law and cases that cross state borders.

≫ PSYCHOMETRY

A psychic power that enables one to "read" the memories attached to an object by touching it. The word "memories" here refers to events involving the object's owner or the places where the object was found. People with this power are called psychometers.

≫ YUZAWAYA

A major arts, crafts, and hobbies store. Primarily found in Kanto. The chain is sixty-two years old.

≫ KODOKU

A type of shamanistic magic derived from ancient Chinese sorcery. A hundred animals and insects are placed into a large pot and forced to eat each other to survive. The last survivor is said to be the strongest, and is used to curse someone. Animals and insects may range in size from as big as snakes to as small as lice.

PARANORMAL SCIENCE NVL

Occultic;Nine

オカルティック・ナイン

THERE IS NO SUCH THING AS THE "OCCULT." IT CAN ALL BE DISPROVED BY SCIENCE.
ONLY THOSE WHO HAVE ACCEPTED EVERYTHING
HAVE THE RIGHT TO KNOW THE TRUTH.

Volume 3 is finally out! I don't even know how many times it's been delayed… in fact, it's been so long that I've forgotten even the fact that it *was* delayed! Just kidding. Just kidding.

I'd like to take this opportunity to apologize to all the fans who were looking forward to the book.

Sorry Sry Sry. (Not a typo).

But you know, I'll come out and say it. This is actually all a "plan," or perhaps you could call it an "experiment."

Yes, this is a trap I have set for all of you.

This book contains a terrifying truth, a thousand times scarier than the anime or the game. I, the author, have discovered it. And for that reason, I've been on the run for the one and a half years this book has been delayed.

Carrying a single notebook.

Yes, this "Aveline Notebook."

The notebook contains a certain fact that will destroy everything we think we know about the world. Something unbelievable, something that will overturn all the value systems that presently exist. But the fact that it's predicted several incidents that occurred in the past means that its contents cannot be denied.

That's how terrifying the Aveline Notebook is.

I needed to protect myself from this terror, no matter what.

Not because I valued my life. No, there was only one reason.

Yes, to tell you all! And there was only one way I could think of to do it.

Yes—to hide the original work. The novel series would stop at Volume 2. The anime would hint at the existence of the notebook.

The last scene of the anime was very suggestive, but it was a wonderful ending that meant something to the people I wanted to understand it.

The manga ran at the same time as the anime. The main characters, themes, and settings were of course the same as the anime, but they were given a degree of freedom to tell the story.

And at last the announcement was made that the original novel would begin, too. At the same time, there was even an announcement of a video game.

Now, which is it? Which is the original work? At this point, you don't even know, do you? Huh? Where is the truth of the Aveline Notebook—no, "The Notebook of Terror"? I needed to hide its location for a while.

That is, until now…

At this point, actually, there's no reason to conceal it any further. There is meaning in publicizing it to the world, and that's something I'd known from the start.

That's why I'm going to tell the truth. And not in the text itself, but in the afterword.

Even "they" won't expect this, and they'll panic when they find out that the truth was hidden in the afterword.

Heheh. It's funny to imagine it. This feels like the first time I've laughed in a long time.

No matter how much they panic, once it's too late, there are limits to what they can do from their world.

Of course, I'm still under powerful electromagnetic attack, so this is a battle where I'm risking my life. But at this point, I've won! It's all thanks to you, the readers, no, my family! Really, thank you.

And I hope you'll keep reading.

Now, are you ready? Are you ready to know the truth? I've got plans for Volume 4, too, so when that happens, make sure you read the afterword, okay? The truth is revealed in the afterword there too, okay? It's such a great idea, isn't it?

Anyway, after that long introduction, it's time for the big reveal. The truth begins here, in the Volume 3 afterword.

Heheh.

Even "they" won't imagine that the truth is hidden in the afterword.

Heheh.

I'm being annoying, aren't I?

Sorry. I'll stop. I will now reveal the information hidden within the Aveline Notebook, no, "The Notebook of Terror"!!!!!! H-huh? Excuse me.

Just a second. I'm getting a phone call. Wait, at this hour? (I'm actually writing in the middle of the night.) I'll pick up, I guess.

Of course, I won't be long. This is important. I'll be right back!

Beep! Bzzztttt zzbbzttt…beep…bzzzzt…

"The bottom of the water… the moonlight… so many people… people people people…"

This will not be uploaded to YouTube

—Chiyomaru Shikura

PARANORMAL SCIENCE NVL

Occultic;Nine

オカルティック・ナイン

THERE IS NO SUCH THING AS THE "OCCULT." IT CAN ALL BE DISPROVED BY SCIENCE.
ONLY THOSE WHO HAVE ACCEPTED EVERYTHING
HAVE THE RIGHT TO KNOW THE TRUTH.